Blaze™

Dear Reader,

We broke one of the cardinal rules in series romance with the first title in our INDECENT PROPOSALS miniseries, *Shameless,* by featuring two heroes. And you clamored for more! You wanted to see Gauge pay for his unapologetic behavior. Moreover, you wanted to understand him and perhaps see him achieve his own unique happy ending.

In *Restless,* he's back! Sexy guitar player Patrick Gauge returns to Fantasy, Michigan, to repair broken bridges, but somehow manages to make things worse instead of better with onetime best friends Nina and Kevin. Meanwhile, just weeks before Christmas, sexy attorney Lizzie Gilbred has been dumped by the man she long believed to be The One, and she is looking for a little something to take her mind off her broken heart. Gauge offers just the sort of temporary solace she needs. But what happens when she wants to make things permanent? Is she woman enough to finally bring this desperado to his knees?

We hope you enjoy every hot, unconventional moment of Gauge and Lizzie's journey toward happily-ever-after. Oh, and if you thought Nina, Kevin and Gauge's story ended in *Shameless*...well, let's just say you've got another think coming.

We'd love to hear from you. Contact us at P.O. Box 12271, Toledo, OH 43612 (we'll respond with a signed bookplate, newsletter and bookmark), or visit us on the Web at www.toricarrington.net.

Here's wishing you love, romance and HOT reading.

Lori and Tony Karayianni
aka Tori Carrington

TORI CARRINGTON
Restless

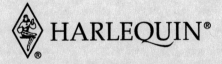

HARLEQUIN®

TORONTO • NEW YORK • LONDON
AMSTERDAM • PARIS • SYDNEY • HAMBURG
STOCKHOLM • ATHENS • TOKYO • MILAN • MADRID
PRAGUE • WARSAW • BUDAPEST • AUCKLAND

Recycling programs
for this product may
not exist in your area.

ISBN-13: 978-0-373-79443-0
ISBN-10:   0-373-79443-6

RESTLESS

www.eHarlequin.com

Printed in U.S.A.

ABOUT THE AUTHOR

Multi-award-winning, bestselling husband-and-wife duo Lori and Tony Karayianni are the power behind the pen name Tori Carrington. Their more than thirty-five titles include numerous Harlequin Blaze miniseries, as well as the ongoing Sofie Metropolis comedic mystery series with another publisher. Visit www.toricarrington.net, www.sofiemetro.com, www.myspace.com/toricarrington and www.eHarlequin.com for more information on the couple and their titles.

We dedicate this book to everyone who wrote demanding Gauge's story. In this increasingly politically correct world it's nice to know that so many agree that a man as flawed as Patrick Gauge warrants a second look and a happy ending all his own. However unconventional...

And to our editor Brenda Chin, for trusting us to push that envelope ever further.

1

THE WEEK-OLD TEXT MESSAGE read: Gone back 2 Jen.
Been nice. Sorry.

Lizzie Gilbred sat on her family-room sofa, clicking
the cell phone to reread the message from her
boyfriend—scratch that, her ex-boyfriend—Jerry, her
thumb hovering over the delete button. It had been seven
days. Surely the words were burned forever into her
brain by now. She saved the message instead, then sighed
and tossed the cell to the leather cushion next to her,
where she knew she'd just pick it up again in two minutes.

She took a hefty sip from her wineglass, leaned her
elbow against the sofa back and stared out the window
at the snow swirling in the yellow security light over her
driveway. The weatherman was calling for three inches
of the white stuff to fall again tonight, casting a festive
glow on the two-week countdown to Christmas.

Blizzard Bill the weatherman's words, not hers. As
far as Lizzie was concerned, they could cancel Christmas this year and she wouldn't even notice.

She took another sip of her wine, feeling a blink

away from jumping out of her skin. She'd returned late from the law offices of Jovavich, Williams, and Brentwood, Attorneys-at-Law, as was usual for a Wednesday, and fought to stick to routine even though she'd felt anything but normal since receiving Jerry's cold text message goodbye. She'd kicked off her shoes at the door, removed her suit jacket, cranked up the heat, poured herself a glass of her favorite Shiraz, started a fire in the family-room grate, then sat on the rich leather sofa she and Jerry had picked out together. Usually at this point she went through her mail or reviewed the briefs or depositions she'd brought home from the office. Tonight it was a brief she'd had one of the junior attorneys write up for her. But damn if she could make it through a single sentence, much less comprehend the entire ten-page document.

She thought about making herself dinner. She hadn't had anything since the bagel with jelly she'd half eaten at the office meeting this morning. But she couldn't seem to drum up the energy to reach for the television remote, much less that required to actually rise from the sofa and go into the kitchen to either heat a frozen dinner or open a can of soup.

So she sat staring out at the snow instead, wondering what her ex-boyfriend, Jerry, and his once-estranged wife, Jenny, were doing right then.

She groaned and rubbed her forehead.

She hadn't thought of Jenny as Jerry's wife in a long time. More specifically, for the past six months—ever since Jerry had left Jenny and appealed for a legal separation. One that had ended with his surprise text message and virtual disappearance from her life a week ago when she'd come home from work after retrieving the missive to find he'd taken everything he'd had at her house, including the waffle maker he'd bought her for her birthday last month.

What did he want with a freakin' waffle maker? Had he taken it to Jenny and said the equivalent of, *Something for you, honey, to show how serious I am about sharing Sunday-morning waffles for the rest of our lives?* Or, *See, I even took back every gift I ever bought her.*

Well, that wasn't entirely true. Because to take back every gift, he'd have had to go back six years, when he and Lizzie were the established couple on the verge of an engagement and Jenny had been the other woman.

God, she couldn't believe she'd let him do this to her again. Six years ago, it hadn't been a text message; rather, he'd left a quickly scribbled note on her car windshield, secured by the wiper: "It's over. Sorry." With it had been the announcement of Jenny and his engagement from that day's newspaper.

The cell phone chirped. Lizzie scrambled to pick it up, punching a button and answering.

"Hello?"

"Lizzie?"

She sank against the cushions and pulled the chenille throw up to her neck. Not Jerry.

"Hi, Mom. How are you?"

"Okay, considering."

Lizzie made a face. Ever since her parents had announced their impending divorce, the War of the Roses Revisited had begun at the Gilbred house. Both of them, it seemed, were all for the separation. But neither was willing to give up the house. So her father had taken up residence in a downstairs guest room, and her mother went about life as if he wasn't there, up to and including a candlelit dinner with some guy she'd picked up at the country club last month.

Her father had had a fit and nearly clunked the guy in the head with one of his golf clubs, which her mother had tossed into the driveway after he'd taken advantage of an unseasonably warm day and gone out for a few rounds, missing an appointment with their divorce attorneys.

The clubs had gone completely missing the following day and Lizzie had gotten a call from her father asking her to help him find them since he'd had the set specially made. They'd finally hit pay dirt at a Toledo pawnshop, where they found them with an abominably low price tag...until the new owner figured out that they must be worth more and jacked up the price while her father fumed.

But maybe her mother was beginning to come to her senses. Usually she began conversations with whatever outlandish thing her father had done that day. That she was actually quiet and appeared pensive was a positive sign. Wasn't it?

"How about you? How are you doing?" her mother asked.

"I'm just sitting in front of the fire with a glass of wine."

"That's nice, dear. And Jerry? Is he there with you?"

She had yet to tell her mother that she and Jerry were no longer a couple. In all honesty, she had never told her parents that he was still married, even though he was legally separated at the time.

What a tangled web we weave, she thought. "Yes. Yes, he is," she lied.

"Hmm? Oh. Yes. Well, tell him hello for me."

"I will."

Lizzie squinted through the window, making out a shadowy, familiar figure in the falling snow.

Gauge.

She instantly relaxed against the cushions. Her hot tenant of the past four months was walking up her driveway, toward the garage and the apartment above it that he was renting. She craned her neck to see around a large evergreen in order to follow his movements until he disappeared.

The voice at the other end of the line sighed.

"Are you okay?" she asked her mother. "You sound…distracted."

Could it be that Bonnie Gilbred was rethinking her situation? That the reconciliation Lizzie, her sister, Annie, and brother, Jesse, hoped for was just around the corner? Just in time to make Christmas feel somewhat like Christmas again?

"Me? Yes, yes. I'm fine. Why wouldn't I be?"

Lizzie nearly dropped the phone when she heard a male roar on her mother's end. She absently rubbed her forehead and closed her eyes, wanting to hang up yet straining to hear her father's words.

"What in the hell did you put in this, Bonnie? Are you trying to kill me, for God's sake? You are, aren't you? Is it arsenic?"

Her mother's voice sounded much too joyful. "No, it's not arsenic, you old fool. I fixed the meat loaf the same way I always fix it. Your taste buds must not be what they once were."

"Don't hand me that *b.s.!*" There was a clatter of plates and then her father cussed a blue streak.

She heard a door slam.

"Mom?" Lizzie said.

"Hmm?"

Apparently Bonnie still had the phone to her ear, but wasn't much paying attention to the fact that she was having a conversation with her daughter.

"What did you put in the meat loaf?" Lizzie asked.

"Salt. Lots of it."

Lizzie smiled in spite of the exasperation she felt. "You know Dad's watching his sodium intake."

"I know. Why do you think I did it?"

Lizzie rested her head back against the pillow. "So is there a reason you called? I mean, other than wanting someone to witness your evildoing for the night?"

"I'm not doing evil. I cooked him meat loaf."

"Sure, Mom. Is there anything else?"

She could imagine Bonnie thinking for a moment. "Nope. I figure that about covers everything."

"Good. Oh, and next time you want a buffer between

you and Dad, call Annie," she said, referring to her younger sister.

"Will do, dear."

"Good night, Mother."

"Good night, Lizzie."

She punched the button to disconnect the call and checked for any missed messages. None. So she read Jerry's text message before tossing the phone to the sofa again.

God, but she really was a sorry sack, wasn't she?

A sound drew her attention back to the driveway. Gauge had reappeared. He was wearing the same hooded sweatshirt and denim jacket he'd had on minutes earlier. She thought maybe he was leaving again. Only he wasn't carrying his guitar case; he was shoveling her walk.

She found the action incredibly hot.

All thoughts of her mother, Jerry and her missing waffle maker drifted from her mind. Replaced by ones related to the sexy drifter who had taken up residence in her garage apartment in August.

His name wasn't really Gauge. Well, his last name was, but his first name was Patrick. Lizzie folded one arm under her chin and took another sip of wine, the alcohol beginning to work its magic by warming her a bit even as she watched Gauge out in the cold.

She didn't know much about him. Her brother Jesse's ex-girlfriend, Heidi, had recommended him; Gauge was part owner of the BMC bookstore café downtown where Heidi used to work. He was a musician. A guitar player, if the case he carried and the strumming she'd heard coming from his place when it was warmer were any indication.

Their paths rarely crossed. She found his rent—always cash—stuffed into an envelope in her front-door mail slot on the first of the month, and she made sure that any mail that was delivered for him was slid under his door.

That was basically it.

Well, that and the fact that he was exceedingly hot and she liked watching him come and go, with no particular preference for either, because both front and back views were worthy of a long glance and an even longer sigh.

She put her glass back down on the coffee table. Aside from a very brief crush on the drummer that had played at her senior prom, she'd never gone much for the artistic type. Career-oriented, driven guys were more her thing.

Like Jerry.

She groaned.

Of course, that was probably because she was a bit on the ambitious side herself. A bit? She needed to stop lying to herself. In three short years since graduation, she'd made it to junior partner at the law firm with a full partnership whispered to be in the offing in the not-too-distant future.

Of course, Jerry's disappearing act wouldn't help. She'd been counting on taking him to the office party next week to help cement her shot at the partnership slot. With, of course, no mention of his marital status.

Her friend Tabitha had suggested that perhaps she should play at being a lesbian. Lizzie had nearly spewed her iced tea at her over lunch at Georgio's, her favorite restaurant in downtown Toledo.

"What did you say?"

Tabby had shrugged. "Surely you know that being an unmarried woman of childbearing age hurts your chances of success in the workplace."

"And acting like a lesbian helps how?"

"For one thing, there's nothing guys like more than imagining a great-looking chick—such as yourself— getting it on with another woman."

Lizzie had snorted.

"For another, they'd be so preoccupied with the image that they'd forget about your biological clock and the fact that you may get pregnant at any minute."

"But there are no kids in my immediate future. The partners know that."

Tabby had given her an eye roll. "Sure. You think they believe you? They know—or think they do—how fickle a woman is. One minute she'll be spouting off about not wanting children, the next she'll be pregnant with quads."

"Don't be ridiculous," Lizzie told her friend.

But Tabitha's advice had made a twisted kind of sense. While she thought she was being treated as an equal at the office, there were small incidents that sometimes left her wondering. Like the men-only golf outings. Or the times she walked into a room full of male colleagues and everyone would go silent.

Then there was Jerry….

He'd been her first love. She had fully expected to

spend the rest of her life with him when they'd met in college and immediately hit it off. It had been that sense of unfinished business, and his convincing argument that she was his first love, as well, that had compelled her to let him back into her life.

What a mistake that had been.

Lizzie forced herself off the couch and downed the remaining contents of her wineglass. That was it. She wasn't going to think about…him, or work or anything anymore for fear that her head might explode.

She craned her neck, watching as Gauge finished the shoveling and headed up the stairs to his place.

No…she shouldn't. To even consider going over there would be nothing but stupid.

Who was she kidding? At that moment it might very well be the smartest decision she'd made in a very long time.

2

GAUGE BRUSHED the snow from his old cowboy boots and shrugged out of his jacket and sweatshirt, hanging them on the back of a kitchen chair in his small studio apartment. He'd hoped the physical activity of shoveling would help chase away the demons that had been haunting him lately. And it had. But for how long?

He grabbed the bottle of Jack Daniel's on the table and unscrewed the top, taking a long pull from the whiskey, standing still as it warmed his chest and then swirled outward to his cold extremities.

The apartment was small but nice. He guessed it had probably been renovated in the past year or so. All the appliances and fixtures were new, the furniture unworn and scratch free. Unlike most of the places he was used to staying in when he was out on the road playing with whatever band he'd hooked up with. Or all the motels rooms, shabby apartments and run-down houses he'd shared with his traveling musician father when he was growing up.

Not that he paid much attention to his surroundings. As far as he was concerned, they were just details. And he probably wouldn't be staying here except for Nina's involvement. Nina was one of his partners in BMC, a bookstore/music center/café, and she matched him up with Lizzie Gilbred, the sister of Heidi's ex, when Lizzie had listed the studio for rent.

He rubbed his chin and screwed the top back on the whiskey, putting the bottle on the table. It wasn't that he didn't like the place. He supposed it was all right. There was just something odd about living in the good part of town. About parking his beat-up Chevy Camaro at the curb where few cars sat, but those that did were BMWs, Mercedes and Rovers. You'd think that he'd be used to the fluttering of curtains as neighbors watched him come and go, but it bothered him on a fundamental level he was loath to ignore. What did they think— that he was going to break in and rape their women? Kill their children?

He didn't know the names of any of them. And he'd lived there for nearly four months. Surely there was something abnormal about that?

Since the places he was used to staying in were shabby, the neighborhoods where they were located tended to be on the grungy side. Usually downtown, crowded with other people that looked like him, where no curtains fluttered because there were usually no curtains. And while he might not stay long in any one place, he always left knowing the names of most of the people around him, and could count more than a few of them as friends.

Hell, here he'd maybe talked to his landlady a handful of times. And she only lived thirty feet away in the Tudor-style monstrosity she called a house. From what he could tell, she used all of three rooms: the kitchen, the back room with the fireplace and what he guessed was her bedroom on the second floor.

He could only imagine what her monthly heating bill looked like.

That's probably why she or any of the other neighbors weren't home much. They were too busy working to pay the bills that went along with their lifestyle—like astronomical heating bills.

Speaking of heat…

After pushing the arrow and nudging the digital numbers up to sixty-nine degrees on the thermostat, he picked up his acoustic guitar where he'd left it sitting on the edge of the queen-size bed and walked around with it until the baseboard heaters warmed the place. He stopped near the window overlooking the driveway. Already the falling snow was beginning to cover his work. He hit a dissonant chord and automatically adjusted the tension of the wayward string, tuning and testing three times before he was satisfied.

His gaze was drawn to the back of the Tudor where he could see Lizzie Gilbred spilled across the leather sofa in front of the fireplace. He ran his fingers over the guitar strings, playing the distinctive licks of Muddy Waters's "Going Down Slow," the sound making the room feel not so empty. There was a time when he might have brought one of the young women who liked his playing home to warm his bed, but not now. Not since he'd come back to Fantasy, determined to forge a different life for himself.

Not since he'd fallen for a woman he'd had no right falling for. A woman he could never have. A woman who was now married to his best friend.

Gauge closed his eyes and dropped his chin to his chest, his fingers moving as if on their own accord.

There had been times lately when he'd thought maybe returning to Michigan hadn't been such a great idea. But in his lifetime, the three-year span he'd spent here was the longest he'd spent anywhere. And when he'd left, he'd been even more aware of the hollow loneliness of wandering the country in search of his next gig than he'd ever been before. Partly because he'd gotten a taste of what love, real love, might be like. Mostly because his best friends and business partners, Nina Leonard and Kevin Weber, had been the family he'd never had.

Until he went and mucked things up.

He forced all thought from his mind, giving himself over to the music, feeling the blues wash over him, through him.

A knock at the door.

Gauge opened his eyes, convinced he was hearing things, because it was a sound he hadn't heard since moving in.

Another knock.

He leaned the guitar against the bed.

He wasn't sure what he expected when he opened the door. But it sure wasn't what he found.

Lizzie Gilbred.

Hadn't he just seen her in her house? What was she doing out in this weather? What was she doing knocking at his door?

She bounced a couple of times, as if cold, looking smaller somehow in the oversize camel-hair coat she wore.

Gauge had always had a deep appreciation of women. He supposed it came from not having had a constant female presence in his life. But the opposite sex never failed to fascinate him. Even if that weren't the case, Lizzie Gilbred would have made a lasting impression on him. It was more than her golden-blond hair and wide, baby-doll-blue eyes. There was an inherent sexiness to her, and he couldn't help wondering why she covered it up in her strict business suits and pulled-back hairstyles.

He couldn't help thinking that if she hadn't been an attorney, she'd have made a great stripper.

"Can I come in?" she asked, intruding on his thoughts.

Probably a bad idea in a long line of bad ideas. Just as he appreciated women, he knew them better than they sometimes knew themselves. And he knew that for whatever reason, Lizzie had decided to distract herself with him.

Then again, his girl-dar had been off a little lately. She could be there to evict him.

Gauge shrugged and moved away from the door. "Seeing as you own the place, I don't know that I can stop you."

She stepped inside, quickly closing the door after her. She looked around the apartment and then at him. "Am I interrupting something?"

Gauge tucked his thumbs into the front pockets of his jeans. Definitely there to distract herself.

Where once the thought might have mildly amused him, now he was vaguely disappointed. But never let it be said that he ever turned a great-looking woman away from his bed. And Lizzie was absolutely stunning. She'd let her coat hang open and he appreciated the snug black cashmere sweater and clingy black pants she wore.

"Am I late with the rent?" he asked.

She smiled. "No. I just thought I'd come up to thank you for shoveling the snow."

"Mmm."

"May I?" she asked, indicating her coat.

"Be my guest."

She shrugged out of the heavy wool coat and draped it over the back of the same chair that held his jacket. She eyed the bottle on the table.

Gauge watched her closely. He knew she was an attorney and that she worked hard. She drove a convertible Audi that was wasted during Michigan's harsh winters. He guessed that her boyfriend was similarly ambitious with his late-model Porsche and fancy suits.

He'd thought it odd that he hadn't seen the jerk's car for the past week. He'd figured maybe the guy had gone on a business trip. Apparently he'd been wrong.

"You want something to drink?" he asked.

"Sounds good."

"Anything in particular?"

"Whatever you're having is fine."

He wasn't entirely sure that was a good idea, but hell, it had been a while. And though he was able to resist tempting any women home, having one offer herself up on his doorstep…well, he was but a man, after all. And it was obvious that's what Lizzie was counting on.

"Boyfriend away?" he asked as he handed her a glass holding a finger of Jack.

Her eyes grew wide and it appeared to take some effort for her to swallow as she drank. "Something like that." She swiped the back of her hand against her mouth. Her lips, he noticed, seemed bare of lipstick. In fact, she didn't appear to be wearing any makeup at all, which was curious. Whenever he'd seen her, she'd always been well put together.

Then again, one didn't require proper attire when slumming it.

And he guessed that's exactly what one sexy Ms. Lizzie Gilbred, trial attorney, was doing. Slumming it. She'd come knocking on his door in need of a quick ego fix. Probably she'd been dumped by that asshole of a boyfriend and needed reminding that she was still desirable.

Then in the morning she'd regret ever crossing that driveway.

But none of that was his concern. The only question was whether he wanted to take what she was offering.

He watched her cross to sit on the edge of his bed

and he raised both of his eyebrows. Most women weren't quite that obvious with their intentions.

"What?" she asked.

He shook his head. "Nothing. Absolutely nothing at all."

LIZZIE LEANED BACK on the bed, on the mattress she had chosen herself for its durability, if not complete comfort, six months ago when she'd moved into the house and had the apartment furnished so she might rent it out. She was acutely aware of the man picking up his guitar and sitting down on the ottoman in front of the chair across the room. Despite the inclement weather, he wore a T-shirt, a dark brown one bearing the logo of a rock band, the hem not quite tucked into jeans that looked like they'd seen their fair share of wild nights out.

She'd always been a sucker for the tall, dark and handsome type, but Patrick Gauge put a whole new spin on the description with his unruly, longish light brown hair and his lanky, rather than athletic, build.

There was something very enticing about the lost-little-boy look. Even though there was definitely nothing boyish about him.

As he ran his long, callused fingers over the guitar strings, she thought that he was waiting for her to say or do whatever she'd come there for.

Instead she silently sipped her whiskey and took her fill of him while he was otherwise occupied. Watching his biceps flex with his movements. The pull of the denim against his groin. The thickness of his neck above the frayed collar of his T-shirt. God, he was rough.

He kept a neat place, she'd give him that. Not overly so—she couldn't detect the scent of any cleaning products—but there wasn't any dirty underwear lying around. Her gaze went back to his groin. Of course, that might be because he didn't wear underwear.

The idea made her hot.

She leaned back farther on the bed, letting the gold liquid creep through her veins, warming her along with the glass of wine she'd had at her place.

She shouldn't be there. Shouldn't be tempting fate along with her tenant. But when she'd glimpsed the rest of the night gaping before her like a fathomless pit faced with the choice of checking a cell phone that would never ring or coming over here to see what temporary trouble she could get into, well…this was definitely preferable.

"The quickest way to get over the old guy is to take up with a new guy," her friend Tabitha was fond of saying.

Of course, Lizzie didn't really plan to *take up* with Gauge. She merely wanted to indulge in something she never had before. More specifically, she wanted to experience a one-night stand. Find out for herself why they were so popular. Any risks involved would be offset by her psychological need to escape her thoughts, if only for a few precious hours.

"Are you playing at the pub this weekend?" she asked, conscious of the way his fingers stroked the strings with the finesse of a pro.

He nodded and then leveled that intense musician's gaze at her. "I'm surprised."

"By what?"

"I didn't peg you as a pub kind of woman."

She smiled. "I take it women don't surprise you often."

"No. Not often."

She watched the way his thick, long fingers manipulated the strings, noticing that the acoustic guitar was old. Two newer guitars—another acoustic, one electric—sat in stands nearby. Scratches marred the front of the one he held, and there even appeared to have been some patchwork down one side.

He played a few more chords, then switched the CD player on.

"Had that long?" Lizzie asked.

He blinked as if seeing the guitar for the first time. He rested the bottom on the floor and moved it so she could see the back. Dozens of words were engraved in the wood. "This guitar shows all the places I've traveled, cities, towns." He turned it back around. "Wherever my guitar is, my heart is."

He leaned the instrument against the ottoman and rested his elbows on his knees, making no secret of his interest in her where she half lay on his bed.

"Are you sure you want to do this?" he asked, his voice as quiet as his playing.

Direct. She liked that.

"Mmm. I'm absolutely positive."

3

GAUGE HAD LEARNED A long time ago that the touch of a woman could be as intoxicating as any liquor. And while Lizzie Gilbred might emerge more Chivas Gold to his Jack, she was an intoxicant all the same as she slid farther back onto the bed, stretching out like a supple black cat with blond hair.

"You don't talk much, do you?" she asked quietly.

His answer was a shake of his head.

"I am. A talker, I mean."

Gauge reached down and took off his right boot, then followed with his left.

He watched her watch him.

"I guess it goes along with the territory. You know, my being a trial attorney. When you come up against opposing counsel, you had better be a pretty good debater."

Gauge took off his T-shirt. He wondered how much debating she'd done before she'd crossed the snow-covered driveway from her large house to his small apartment. Had she considered all the angles? Taken in the possible consequences?

For reasons he couldn't quite name, he had the feeling that she hadn't. Something, some event, had pushed her to come to his place on the spur of the moment. And his silent disrobing across the room from her was his way of giving her a chance to change her mind.

He lowered his hands toward the fly of his jeans and paused. Instead of scooting toward the end of the bed in order to make her exit, sexy Lizzie Gilbred ran her pink tongue along her lips, her gaze riveted to his actions.

Let it not be said that he hadn't given her ample opportunity to hightail it out of there. Realize that what she was about to do was something she couldn't take back or erase.

He crossed the room and sat on the edge of the bed.

"You have a great physique," she said quietly, reaching out to run her fingertips down his right arm. "Must be the guitar playing."

Gauge shifted to face her, taking her hands and bringing her to a sitting position. She appeared ready for him to kiss her. Instead he reached for the hem of her sweater and slowly brought it up, purposely avoiding meeting her lips. This wasn't about intimacy—it was about sex. Pure and simple. An escape as stimulating as spirits. He tugged the soft material over her head, tousling her golden hair and revealing that she was every bit as shapely as he'd suspected. A bloodred satin bra did what his palms were suddenly itching to do, namely curve under the fleshy orbs of her breasts.

He skimmed his fingers over the glossy material and she inhaled deeply.

Gauge looked into her eyes to find a mixture of fascination and curiosity on her beautiful face.

Her tongue made a repeat performance. "Don't you think we should turn out the lights?"

Two lamps filled the room with dim light, and he didn't want to switch off either one of them.

He pretended not to hear her as he slid both of his hands over the satin cups until his hands supported her as much as her bra. He rubbed his callused thumbs over the firm tips, scratching the delicate material.

He'd never understood a woman's desire for shiny lingerie. To him, there was nothing sexier than a naked woman. Her soft skin, fleshy curves, shadowy crevices. Nothing man-made could ever rival the sight of a woman's trembling stomach, or the cleft between her legs.

He worked his thumbs inside the bra cups until her taut nipples popped out of the top.

Lizzie's breathing quickened, but she didn't move, apparently content to let him take command.

Gauge took one of the nipples into his mouth, reveling in the feel of the stiff, puckered skin against his tongue. She smelled like a mixture of cucumbers and musk. She tasted like heaven. He squeezed the soft flesh with his fingers and took in more of her, sucking deeply. She gasped and grasped his wrist, as if unsure whether to pull him away or urge him closer.

Gauge took the decision away from her by removing his mouth and reaching behind her to undo the clasp of her bra. The flimsy material instantly gapped forward and he helped her the rest of the way out of it, ignoring her attempts to kiss him.

He reached for the catch to her slacks even as she

fumbled with his zipper. Gauge stretched out next to her to make the transition easier. He felt her mouth on his shoulder and neck, hot, hungry, even as he clenched his back teeth and sought the springy curls between her legs with his fingers…only to find… She was completely bare, her flesh as smooth as the satin of her bra.

He groaned in the back of his throat, his erection immediately standing up at attention at the sight of her womanhood looking like a ripe fruit just waiting to be tasted.

And taste it he did….

LIZZIE'S BACK CAME UP off the mattress at the feel of Gauge's hot mouth between her legs.

Oh, dear…

She couldn't remember the last time someone had gone down on her. Keen awareness exploded through her, robbing her breath, making her aware of every swirl of his tongue, every beat of her heart.

Oh, yes. This definitely had been a good idea.

She forced her eyes open and tucked her chin into her chest so she could watch Gauge's dark head as he parted her legs, baring her fully to his gaze. He followed the line of her fissure with his thumbs then opened her fleshy lips, his tongue lapping at her most intimate of intimates.

She was suddenly incapable of swallowing, incapable of thought. She twisted her fists into the downy blanket under her, reaching for something, anything that would relieve the pressure building between her legs…in her veins…filling her stomach. It seemed as if she'd flown too close to the sun in one long catapult, needing to pull away, yet wanting to stay to enjoy the spectacular view.

He slid his index finger inside her throbbing depths and she cried out, coming instantly, the pressure escaping in a series of muscle-deep spasms.

She was just beginning to regain her breath when she realized he was still licking her, apparently lapping her clean.

Lizzie found it difficult to swallow, a convert to lights-on sex. She'd been able to watch every expression on his face, every movement of his tongue. She'd been laid out against the mattress, open to his attentions, vulnerable at her weakest moment.

And she'd experienced one of the best orgasms she'd had in recent memory.

Gauge lifted himself up on his arms, his gaze intense as it flicked over her face. He slid forward until his hips lay between her legs and his chest rasped against the tips of her breasts. Lizzie's hands immediately went to his face, needing to draw him near so she could kiss him.

He buried his face in her neck instead, leaving her little choice but to focus her attention on his shoulder.

He was hard where a man was meant to be hard, no extra ounce of flesh on him anywhere. There was a tattoo on his right arm, but she couldn't make it out as she felt him move between her thighs.

Her throat tightened when she felt him naked and hard against her slick portal.

"Condom?" she choked.

He didn't say anything for a long moment, merely ran his mouth against the column of her neck, creating a wet trail down to her breast and back.

What if he refused to wear one? Sure, she was on the pill, mostly to help regulate her periods, but she'd even made Jerry wear a condom.

"In the drawer to your right," he said quietly.

Relieved, she reached for and found a foil-wrapped packet, freeing the lubricated latex inside and helping to sheath him. When he might have pulled away to enter her, she wrapped her fingers around his thick width instead and measured his length. Her thumbnail barely reached her index fingernail around him, and she guessed that if he got hard in his jeans and his member was positioned upward, you might see the tip there at the waist. Because she'd been right in her earlier supposition that he didn't wear briefs or boxers.

Nice…

He held himself above her, watching her face, his own cast in shadow from his tousled dark hair. His mouth was incredible, his lips generous, almost feminine. She released his erection and licked her lips in preparation for his kiss.

He entered her in one slow stroke instead.

She'd thought his mouth had worked miracles, but that had left her woefully unprepared for the feel of him inside her.

She was almost too tight for him, too small. But as he waited for her slick muscles to adjust to his size, a hungry restlessness built within her. She bent her knees for better traction and tilted her hips upward, taking even more of him in.

She blindly sought his mouth and connected with his jaw instead, kissing him repeatedly as he slowly withdrew and then slid inside her again, filling her almost to overflowing.

"Kiss me!" she whispered, grasping his arms to steady herself for his quickened stroke.

He did. He kissed her cheek nearer her ear. Then he whispered back, "This is fucking, Lizzie. Not lovemaking. It's best that neither of us gets confused."

Then he quickened the pace of his strokes more, giving her little time to protest or to even consider protesting as he shoved her closer and closer to her next climax….

THE FOLLOWING MORNING, Gauge woke to the sound of a ringing phone. Probably one of the neighbors', he thought, rolling onto his back and pulling the pillow over his head. Then he realized that he didn't have any neighbors. At least not ones separated from him by a wall.

He dragged the pillow off his face and stared at the ceiling, guessing it to be around nine or ten. The scent of musk teased his nose and he put the pillow back to his face, glancing at the other side of the bed. Gone.

It was just as well that Lizzie Gilbred had gotten up and left his place at some point during the night.

He reached for the telephone receiver next to the bed, but it stopped mid-ring.

Good.

He reached down and scratched his balls then slid his fingers down his semierect shaft. He'd give Lizzie a lot of credit. Some women might have taken offense at his refusal of intimacy. Not her. If anything, she'd seemed further turned-on by the idea that she was there for sex and sex only. No strings that stretched beyond the perimeter of this bed.

She'd been insatiable. Going from screaming orgasm one moment to frenzied, sex-starved nympho the next. It had been a good long while since he'd enjoyed more than just a ten-minute sack session with a woman.

And months since he'd awakened not thirsting for a swallow from the bottle on the kitchen table across the room.

He tossed off the blankets and rose from the bed, heading for the bathroom and the shower, where he stood for long minutes under the hot spray. He'd promised the band that he'd stop by the pub this morning to practice before they opened for lunch. He shouldn't have a problem making it, seeing as he really didn't have anything else on his agenda.

Hell, he didn't know what he was still doing in Fantasy, Michigan. If he'd known what was good for him, he'd have left right after Nina and Kevin's wedding in August. Would never have unpacked his bag or his guitar and would have hightailed it back out after the reception.

But he hadn't.

For some reason he had yet to fully define, he'd

stayed on, renting the garage apartment from sexy Lizzie Gilbred, sitting in with area bands when they needed him and waiting until either wanderlust or a long-term commitment to a single band saw him hitting the road again.

Then he'd blinked and it was almost Christmas.

He'd hoped to be well out of the northern city before winter hit. While he'd lived through the past three when he'd gone into partnership with Nina and Kevin, he'd been vaguely looking forward to heading someplace south this season, as he had done in the years before the three had become friends.

He pushed his face into the punishing hot spray and ran his hands over the stubble covering his jaw.

Friends. Now there was a word for you.

The ringing started again.

Gauge shut off the water and stood dripping, listening to it. When it appeared the caller wasn't about to give up, he grabbed a towel, rubbing it against his hair as he walked into the other room and picked up the extension.

"Gauge?"

His every muscle tightened as he recognized the female voice on the other end. Nina....

4

LIZZIE CLOSED her notepad and stood up from the conference table. The afternoon strategy meeting to discuss a case going to court the following week was drawing to a close.

"I want to see that deposition, Mark," she said to a junior associate.

"It'll be on your desk by tomorrow morning."

"I'd prefer a half hour." She turned toward another associate. "Mary Pat, how's the witness prep going?"

The pretty brunette smiled. "As well as can be expected. I've got another meeting with the key to go over testimony on Friday. Hopefully this time he won't crack under cross."

Lizzie nodded. "If anyone can handle it, you can."

The room began emptying out as everyone said good-night and hurried off before she could assign them another task or ask another question.

Lizzie was the last one out. Which was usually the case. Her boss, John Stivers, had always said she was one of the hardest workers he'd ever seen. And, of course, the instant he'd said it, she'd determined to work even harder.

It was after six and she understood that many of her associates had families they wanted to get home to. The three senior partners had called it a day an hour or so ago, as had the secretarial pool and most of the paralegals, but she'd requested the late meeting because it was the only time they could fit it in.

She entered her office and put her files on her desktop. Her own paralegal was still on the clock and peeked her head through the door leading to the lobby area.

"Do you need me for anything else?" Amanda asked.

Lizzie glanced at her watch, then through the window. It was dark already. The white landscape looked grim from her third-floor office in the new building built to accommodate the expanding practice.

At least five things sprang to mind, but instead she waved her hand. "Go on home, Amanda. I'll see you in the morning."

"Thanks. Good night."

"Good night."

Lizzie sank down into her coffee-colored leather desk chair and sat for long moments, watching as the offices emptied out.

The partners had conducted a survey that estimated there was a more than thirty percent turnover of new attorneys at high-powered law firms nationwide, while their own partnership was doing slightly better, mostly because of the incentive program she'd helped them devise the year before. While Lizzie and a handful of other associates hungry to climb the partnership ladder put in over a hundred hours a week, most of the others averaged between sixty and eighty. Since much of their time as trial attorneys was spent at the courthouse, the only opportunity to do follow-up and file and prep work was after the regular hours of nine-to-five.

By rights, she should be feeling tired. Instead, she found she was still energized. She smiled as she compiled her notes and put a couple of files in her out-box. Over the past week she'd had to mainline caffeine to keep going. Today…

Her eyes widened. Today, she'd barely thought about Jerry and his leaving her high and dry.

Instead, she found her thoughts trailing to one very hot, very sexy Patrick Gauge.

She squeezed her thighs together, feeling tingly all over again.

Her cell phone chirped. She tilted it on her desk so she could read the display and then answered.

"I need a drink. Meet me at Ciao?" Tabitha asked.

Lizzie smiled. She could always count on her old friend to liven things up. If not for Tabitha this past week, things would have been harder than they had been. She and Lizzie had been close ever since attending University of Toledo Law School together, and they'd seen each other through some difficult times.

Despite their shared interest in the legal system, they'd taken different paths. While Lizzie had chosen trial law, Tabby had gone the bankruptcy route, helping strapped people regain some kind of control over their lives.

Lizzie asked now, "Why do you need a drink?"

"You're right. I probably don't need a drink. But I want one." Tabitha sighed. "A long day, that's all."

"Tell me about it," Lizzie agreed, although she hadn't felt the day had been particularly grueling.

"You're sounding better. Oh, no. Don't tell me. He called."

"Who?" she asked, before thinking. She cringed. Tabby knew her much too well not to read the road signs.

"Hmm. Okay. I suppose the question should be, 'who is he'?"

"Who?" Lizzie asked again.

"Ah, yes. She's taking my advice that the best way to forget about the last guy is to find the next." Tabitha laughed, a throaty sound that never failed to make Lizzie smile. "So you're feeling better then."

"I'm feeling better."

"Good. You've been such a train wreck this past week, I was afraid I might have to drag you to an AA meeting or two. Either that, or you might have to drag me."

"Do you mind if I pass for tonight?"

"Mind? Hell, my credit card will thank you. Unlike you, I don't have access to a bottomless expense account."

"Whatever."

"Call me tomorrow?"

"If you don't call me first."

Lizzie signed off after a few more moments and then sat back in her chair, both glad Tabby hadn't asked again about the man who had taken her mind off Jerry and disappointed. Given the one-night nature of her liaison with

Gauge, a part of her wanted to keep it private. Still, it had been so good, it was nearly impossible not to share.

While she'd never considered herself a good girl, she'd never really been a bad one, either. One-night stands were better left to those who had the time to waste. She'd been so focused first on school, then at the firm, that it was all she could do to stop by her parents' a couple of times a week before dropping into bed at night, exhausted, only to start the cycle over again the next day.

She shifted her watch around on her wrist and looked at the pearly face, even though she knew what time it was. What she was really doing was wondering what Gauge was up to.

She was pretty sure the band played only on the weekends…which meant he should be home.

A warm pool of longing filled her stomach.

God, how long had it been since she'd experienced this heightened awareness? It was too long ago to remember her first time with Jerry. Had she felt the same way? She figured she must have, because she'd fallen in love with him all those years ago. Enough that she hadn't hesitated to take him back six months ago, seeing his return as the fulfillment of what they'd begun all those years ago but never finished.

Or perhaps it had been her own competitive spirit that had made her open that door to him again. After all, stealing him away from his wife was a kind of vindication of their earlier relationship.

She opened her desk drawer and took out her purse. So much for not thinking about Jerry.

But for the first time in days she felt she had a choice in the matter.

THE TENSION at the Weber dining-room table was palpable, with Nina either ignorant of the unspoken words exchanged between the two men…or overly aware of them. Gauge couldn't decide which.

He knew he shouldn't have come. But over the past few months he'd turned down her every invitation to dinner at their place, preferring to meet them in public and avoid what he knew was a need for a showdown of sorts that had been brewing since last February. He'd known he'd have to accept at some point, and now was as good a time as any.

If only Kevin wasn't slanting him looks that said he'd like nothing better than to pummel him to a pulp right there and then.

When Gauge had returned for Nina and Kevin's wedding in August, his long absence had allowed for a lowering of defenses and he'd gladly taken the spot beside Kevin as his best man. But later that day at the reception, Gauge had pushed his luck when he'd asked for a dance with the bride…and found himself right back at square one with his one-time best friend.

Gauge focused on his surroundings now. He was familiar with the house. Kevin had inherited it from his late parents, and Gauge had been there no fewer than a couple of dozen times. Still, it had undergone such intensive renovations he barely recognized it.

"Place looks good," he said, noticing that the wall between the kitchen and dining room had been knocked out, giving an airier feel. "Amazing what a woman's touch will do."

He purposely looked at Kevin, hoping to lighten the atmosphere. But the problem was that Nina had touched them both, in more ways than one.

Nina cleared her throat as she spooned gravy over the thin slices of brisket on his plate. "Actually, Kevin is the one who deserves complete credit."

Gauge narrowed his gaze on her as the couple shared a glance.

"I tore the place up after..." Kevin began, then looked at Gauge pointedly.

Gauge picked up his fork. It seemed everything he said led back to that one night.

"I didn't move in until after we married," Nina said, taking the seat across from him and sliding her hand over Kevin's. He sat at the head of the table between them. "Kevin wanted me to, but I preferred to wait until we got married."

Gauge glanced into the living room, where the gift he'd bought them hung on the wall between the front windows and the door. An authentic dream catcher made by the Ojibwa Indians. It had seemed like a good idea at the time. It would be great if it could really filter out all the bad and leave only the good.

He forked the mashed potatoes and put a bite into his

mouth. He'd been stupid to think he could just come back. That the three of them could take up where they'd left off before that fateful night when Nina had agreed to allow him and Kevin to fix her up with a blind date. More specifically they'd blindfolded her, and she hadn't known which of the two she'd slept with.

The food tasted like sawdust in his mouth. He reached for his water glass to help wash it down.

"So, do you know when you might come back to work at BMC?" Nina asked.

Kevin's fork screeched against his plate and Gauge looked at him. He got the distinct impression that his old friend would like nothing better than for Gauge to just walk out of town and never come back.

Of course, that's not how he'd felt when Gauge had returned at Nina's request for their August wedding. Kevin had hugged him like a long-lost brother. And in that one moment, he'd been glad he'd come back. Been reminded of the deep bond of friendship he'd shared with the other man.

Unfortunately, that's not the only thing they'd shared.

He looked over at Nina.

God, but she was as beautiful as ever. Like a brilliant desert rose whose fragrance he could smell across the table. Her blond hair had grown out a bit from the way she'd once worn it, but it still hung in a shiny curtain around her pretty face. She had on a clingy red, long-sleeved shirt and black pants that hugged her curves in all the right places. It looked like she'd put on a few pounds, and they suited her. Her breasts were a little larger, her bottom high and shapely.

He picked up his knife and started to cut the meat. Only it refused to be cut.

All three of them appeared to be doing the same thing at once. And no one was having any luck.

"Sorry…the beef seems a little on the tough side," Nina murmured.

He watched as Kevin folded a piece onto his fork. "I like big bites anyway."

Gauge grinned, watching him put the food into his mouth and chew. And chew.

He followed suit, folding the slice of meat with the help of his knife and then putting it into his mouth.

It tasted like the belt that held up his jeans. Or what he imagined that must taste like.

The three of them chewed until finally Nina spit the contents of her mouth into her napkin, her cheeks turning an attractive shade of red.

"Mmm," Kevin said. "It's…delicious, honey."

Gauge had to give him credit for swallowing what must have felt like an entire boot in one gulp. Since Kevin had already drained his glass of water, Gauge pushed his own mostly filled glass his way. His friend gave him a look of gratitude as he downed nearly the entire contents.

A sound came from Nina's direction. Gauge and Kevin looked to see her eyes bright with tears. Gauge discreetly spit his own bite into his napkin and followed Kevin's lead.

"It's the best home-cooked meal I've had in a long time."

Only it hadn't been tears of exasperation that sparkled in her bright blue eyes; rather they were inspired by laughter.

Nina grinned. "That's because you probably haven't had a home-cooked meal in so long you've forgotten what it tastes like."

Kevin coughed into his napkin. "Actually, that depends on what home you're talking about. Because in this house, this is what a home-cooked meal tastes like."

Laughter burst from the table and created a happy cloud around the three of them that had been sorely missing.

Gauge was glad for the change.

Nina stopped laughing first. "God, I'm sorry. I followed the recipe to a T. I don't have a clue what happened."

She picked up Kevin's plate and forked the meat back into the serving dish.

"Don't touch my mashed potatoes," he said. "I love your mashed potatoes."

Gauge felt suddenly like an outsider. Which was something he was getting used to when in the presence of his two friends. He could accept them being a married couple. But he still hadn't figured out how to deal with it.

Especially since he couldn't seem to stop himself from wanting what Kevin had. Namely, Nina.

"I should stick to café fare," she said. "Soups and sandwiches I can handle."

"Don't forget baking," Kevin reminded.

"Yeah. So long as you don't mind living on bear

claws, I suppose I'm your dream mate." She rolled her eyes, but her warm smile belied her true feelings as she handed him back his plate. "I'm going to go order pizza. You two clear the table."

An hour and a half later, Gauge picked up the empty pizza boxes while Kevin went to change the CD in the player in the living room. He took the boxes into the kitchen, where Nina was opening another bottle of wine.

"Thanks," she said as he passed behind her on the way to the garbage bin.

"You want some help with that?"

She let out a long sigh. "I swear, I've never been any good at popping corks."

Before he could weigh the wisdom of the move, he curved both of his arms around her, pressing his front against her soft, hot bottom. "It's simple. You just have to remember to keep the corkscrew in perfect line with the bottle."

Damn, but she smelled good. Like warm, summer sunshine. A field full of wildflowers. Like rain against a hot sidewalk.

With his help, she popped the cork.

"Oh!" she said, and he heard her swallow.

It satisfied him on a level he was loath to admit that his close proximity still affected her.

Suddenly she went stiff against him. Gauge looked up to find Kevin standing in the kitchen doorway, his fists looking like meat mallets on either side of his legs.

"Get the hell away from my wife."

5

MERELY DRIVING UP to her parents' house filled Lizzie with memories of the past, and bittersweet thoughts of the present. Her parents had been the family's foundation, their rock. How could they even consider getting divorced now? After thirty years of marriage? It didn't make sense.

Lizzie let herself in through the back door, much as she had for nearly the entire twenty-eight years of her life. The house was one of the first that her father had built after opening his own construction company before she was born. While he'd added on to it over the years to accommodate her mother's wishes for a sunporch and her brother's for a media room, much remained the same. Decor aside, of course. Her mother claimed that she'd been Martha Stewart before Martha even thought about making her first pinecone wreath. The house had undergone a complete makeover nearly every year, with a change in color schemes and throw rugs and artwork.

Now the living room walls were a soft, homey green, which went well with the upholstered furniture, a cream color festooned with tiny flowers of every color. The furniture had remained the same, chosen because it went with almost everything. Photos of the family, especially the three children, dotted the walls and mantel, documenting the various stages of their lives.

"Mom?" Lizzie called out, putting her purse on the kitchen table and shrugging out of her coat, much as she had countless times before. Only this time there was no answer.

She hadn't checked the garage to see if either of their cars was there. It was usually a given at this time of night that her parents would both be home. It was just after dinner and right about now they normally would have been sitting at the kitchen table enjoying coffee and dessert or in the family room watching the news or reading.

The silence seemed to verify with deafening intensity that nothing was normal or usual anymore.

Lizzie sighed and looked around the kitchen. When she was growing up, there had always been something to eat. It was one of the many reasons neighborhood children had liked to hang out there. If there wasn't a pot of something on the stove to sample, there were surely sandwich fixings and a bag of chips somewhere.

The sink was empty, the stove barren and not even the cookie jar held a crumb to lick off the pad of her finger. She opened the refrigerator. Bingo. She smiled as she popped the lid on a container of food and took out a slice of meat loaf.

She sputtered when an overdose of salt assaulted her taste buds.

She moved to the sink and coughed up the meat, running the water to wash it down the drain as she tripped the trash compactor.

"Damn," she muttered under her breath, having forgotten the phone call of the night before.

She dumped the rest of the "poisoned" meat loaf into the garbage can and placed the container in the dishwasher.

She should have known the situation had deteriorated to this degree, but the absence of broken glass littering the floor had convinced her that things were as they always had been.

She opened the freezer and took out a fudge pop, visually verifying that no tampering had taken place. She hesitantly licked it, sighed with relief and then closed the freezer door. Do what you will with the meat loaf, she thought, but leave anything chocolate alone.

Of course, her father didn't like chocolate.

Sucking on the sweet, she left the kitchen, walking through the hall toward the foyer. She immediately spotted her mother's purse on the table near the door.

Huh?

"Dad?"

She stepped down the connecting hall toward the guest room that had once been a den and then a guest room again and rapped lightly on the closed door. No answer. She peeked inside to see the sofa bed open, the sheets and blanket unmade, and then closed the door again.

So her father wasn't there. But her mother?

A sound from the second floor.

Maybe her mother was taking a bath with her headphones on and hadn't heard her.

While the Gilbreds weren't immodest, rare were the times when a bathroom door was locked. Lizzie had spent many a time sitting on the closed commode talking to her mother while Bonnie was immersed in a tub full of bubbles.

Of course, when those same bubbles started to dissipate, she was the first to give her mother privacy…and to spare herself from viewing something that might ruin her for life.

She climbed the stairs, licking her frozen treat as she went. She supposed she could grab a sandwich on the way home. Or see if the Chinese place on Oak Street was still open.

She looked first in the master bedroom to find everything perfectly in its place, the bed made, the connecting bath empty.

Okay…

Had her mother left her purse behind? Was she even now eating out somewhere and reaching for her wallet, only to find she'd left it at home on the foyer table? That was so unlike her mother as to be scary.

Scarier still was the fact that both her parents constantly requested that she act as their attorney. She was grateful she wasn't a family attorney and was only too quick to point that out whenever the topic raised its ugly head. Which was much too often for her liking.

She checked out the main bathroom just to make sure her mother wasn't in there, then shrugged and

headed to her old room. Bonnie had kept all the kids'
bedrooms decorated the same way as when they'd lived
at home, the wallpaper a little harder to change than the
color of paint. Lizzie sometimes liked to go into her old
room and lie across her white canopy bed, remembering happier times.

Another sound.

Lizzie's footsteps slowed. If she wasn't mistaken, it
had come from her old room.

She slowly opened the door and then gasped, standing rooted to the spot. Lying across her old bed was her
mother, naked, her hands tied above her head to the
canopy posts. Her father was kneeling at the edge, an
extra large feather held aloft as he swung his head to
look at her.

And the sound? The headboard hitting the wall.

Lizzie screamed and ran from the room. So much for
leaving a scene before it ruined her for life. She didn't
think she'd ever be able to go into her old bedroom again.

A COUPLE HOURS LATER, Lizzie sat on the leather couch
in her family room, flipping through channels on the
television, purposely ignoring her vibrating cell phone.
Her mother had called no fewer than five times since
Lizzie had bolted from the house as if the floor had been
covered with burning coals. Much of what had happened
since the moment she'd caught her parents playing Pin
the Princess on her bed—her childhood bed in her childhood room—had passed in a blur. She couldn't even remember what she'd done with the fudge pop.

And at this point, she didn't care, either. She half hoped she'd dropped the melting chocolate on the white carpet of her old room so her mother would have to clean it up…among other things.

Ugh.

Well, she supposed there was one good thing to come out of the situation. Her parents appeared to have reconciled.

She stuck her chopsticks into the rice container and put both down on the coffee table, pulling the chenille throw across her lap up to her chin.

Her cell vibrated and she turned the display so she could read the caller ID. Her sister, Annie.

She answered.

"Okay, what's up? Mom's going out of her mind with worry because you aren't taking her calls."

Leave it to Annie to cut straight to the chase.

Younger than Lizzie by a year, her sister usually managed to keep up the front that her life was all sunshine and roses. But Lizzie knew it was more like dirty diapers and teething rings. The last time she'd talked to Annie, her sister had been a scant inch removed from running away from her family altogether. Which didn't make any sense to Lizzie, because so far as she could tell, her sister had gotten everything she'd ever wanted out of life. A great husband. A marvelous house. Two beautiful children and another on the way.

Not that little Jasmine and Mason were angels. Far from it. They were loud and smelly and needed constant supervision. And somewhere in there, Annie had to fit in love, as well. Which wasn't always easy.

So Lizzie and Annie had spent a lot of time on the phone lately. The approach suited Lizzie fine. Since she worked such long hours, she wasn't physically able to step in to help her sister out much. The issue of children in her own future still hung like a swaying question mark. Not because she'd had any bad experiences or her sister's situation had turned her off kids. She'd simply been so busy she hadn't had a chance to think about them.

That, and she had yet to meet a man she loved enough to consider sharing another human being with.

Even Jerry.

So Lizzie paid back her sister's brevity with a concise rundown of the evening's events.

A silent pause stretched after she finished. Then, finally, Annie's laughter filled her ear.

Lizzie scooted down farther into the sofa. "I'm glad to be a source of comic relief."

In truth, her sister's response irritated her.

"Tied to your bed…a feather? Oh my God, Liz, this is classic Mom and Dad."

"Yeah, maybe. But not when they were in the middle of a divorce."

"Maybe."

Another silence as both considered a future in which their parents weren't married. Fractured holidays spent running from one parent's house to the other, never satisfying either of them, always hearing a litany of the ex-spouse's flaws.

They'd both seen it happen to friends. And it was a way of life they'd counted themselves lucky not to have to confront.

There was a brief cry at the other end of the line. Lizzie realized her sister must have been holding Mason, her youngest.

"Shh," Annie said soothingly.

Surprisingly, the sound served to make Lizzie feel better.

"Remember the time we caught them going at it in the garage in the middle of the day?" Annie asked.

Lizzie groaned. "Did you have to remind me of that occasion? I mean, my God, we were like, what? All of ten and eleven? And we had friends with us."

"I forgot about that. But what I can see clearly is Mom with her tennis skirt hiked up around her hips sitting on the washing machine, Dad's shorts down around his ankles, the two of them going at it during the spin cycle."

Lizzie rubbed her forehead. "Or how about the time they took us to the drive-in when we were even younger than that?"

"Oh, God! And they started going at it right there in the front seat, thinking the three of us were asleep in the back."

"Yes, well, if we had been, the squeaking of the car springs would have woken us."

"If Mom's shouts hadn't."

They shared a laugh. "Well, you can't say that it hasn't been an interesting run."

"No, that you can't. But what I don't understand is

why, after all these years, the two would even contemplate divorce."

Lizzie worried her bottom lip. "Maybe they ran out of places to do it?"

"There's that."

"Have you really talked to either of them about it?" Lizzie asked.

"Me? Are you kidding? I'm almost afraid to ask, what with all I've got going on." Mason made a few cooing sounds. "How about you?"

"No. I mean, I tried a couple of times. But the two of them seem so caught up in the act of divorcing that my questions hit a wall."

"What about Jesse? Do you think he's talked to them?"

Lizzie didn't even bother answering. Jesse was going through an interesting time of his own, what with dumping the girl he'd been engaged to practically since junior year of high school for a pole dancer from Boston.

"Maybe it's time we called a family meeting," Lizzie suggested instead.

"A what?"

"You know, make an appointment for all of us to come together so we can talk this out."

"I don't know if that's such a good idea. Think about it, Liz. You can't handle the idea of them still having an active sex life—"

"I can handle the idea of them having sex…I just don't want to view it."

"Anyway, do you really want to hear what's driven them apart? All the gritty details?"

"Somebody's got to."

Annie sighed. "Yeah, well, after today, let's hope there's nothing more to worry about. Let's hope they've worked out their differences and that life goes back to normal again so Christmas can go ahead as scheduled."

Lizzie dropped her head back against the couch and closed her eyes. "I forgot all about Christmas."

"I finished my shopping yesterday."

"Shocker. I haven't started."

"Shocker. What are you going to get Mom and Dad?"

"How about an appointment with a shrink?"

"Ha-ha. No, really."

"I have no idea, Annie," she said quietly, considering all that had happened that night. Hell, over the course of the past week.

She didn't ask her sister what she'd gotten them. Annie always had a great handle on the perfect gift for everyone.

"Okay, I'd better put Mason down. Do you want me to call Mom? Or will you?"

"I'll call her in the morning."

"Fine, I'll call her now."

"Do what you will."

"Good night, Lizzie."

"What's good about it, Annie?"

Her sister laughed and signed off.

Lizzie pressed the disconnect button and tossed the cell phone to the other side of the sofa. She nearly jumped out of her skin when she heard a light tap on the patio windows behind her.

She jerked around to find Gauge standing outside holding up what looked like a mug of something.

Hmm…

6

"GET THE HELL AWAY from my wife."

The words seemed burned into Gauge's mind, the three hours since he'd heard them doing nothing to diminish their effect.

There he'd been, standing in Kevin and Nina's kitchen, his arms around Nina from behind, helping her to open a fresh bottle of wine. Yes, he had maybe stood a little too close. Yes, he'd sniffed her hair as if he'd like nothing more than to bury his nose there. Yes, he'd felt her bottom, hot and hard against his promising arousal. But he would never have pushed things any further.

As he stood on Lizzie's back steps waiting for her to open the kitchen door, he called himself the liar he knew himself to be.

Nina had been the one to hold up her hands. "Please, Kevin, let's not ruin what's turning out to be a perfectly nice evening."

Gauge had moved away from her, but not quickly enough, it appeared, because Kevin looked a scant breath removed from delivering the pummeling his expression promised.

In a fair fight, Gauge might have been able to take him. But there was nothing fair about a man in love, afraid his best friend was making a move on his woman. Gauge got that.

What Gauge didn't get was why he had done what he had. Beyond it seeming like a purely innocent act at the time.

There had, however, been absolutely nothing innocent in his reaction. Or in the hitch in Nina's breathing. And he knew that if he could have taken it further, he would have.

The door opened suddenly in front of him and he grimaced, forgetting for a moment where he was. What he was doing.

Until Lizzie's provocative face filled his line of vision.

He found himself grinning. A natural grin, despite the night's awkward events.

Nina had tried to force an air of normalcy on the last hour of his visit, but there had been nothing normal about eating dessert in the living room of a man who would just as soon Gauge disappeared from the face of the earth.

As Nina had uncomfortably kissed him good-night—a peck on the cheek that he wished would have lingered a little longer—she'd smiled and said, "I think it's a good first step."

First step toward what? He'd wondered. A first step toward resurrecting a friendship among the three of them that was better left to wither away?

He'd heard it said over the years that platonic friendship between a man and a woman was impossible. That sex always managed to get in the way. And he'd believed it. Until he'd met Kevin and Nina. For three years they'd been friends, as well as business partners. For three years they'd enjoyed a nonsexual, if flirtatious, relationship.

Then he'd found a way to screw even that up.

"Gauge?"

He focused again on the woman in front of him.

Lizzie.

She pulled her sweater a little closer.

"Do you want to come in?" she asked.

He stepped through the open doorway, allowing her to close the door after him.

"Hi," she said, coming to stand back in front of him.

There was a lot in her expression he couldn't read.

He lifted the empty coffee cup he held. "I was hoping to borrow some sugar."

She laughed, a happy sound that made him feel slightly better. "Do people really do that? Borrow sugar, I mean? I thought that was just something that happened in the movies."

"Or back when there wasn't a corner market open twenty-four/seven."

She didn't make a move to take the cup, merely stood looking at him as if curious about more than the questions she'd asked.

"Are you okay?" she asked quietly.

Gauge squinted at her. Was there something in his appearance that indicated that he wasn't all right? That spoke of what he was going through?

Something that Lizzie had picked up on?

He wasn't sure how he felt about that. Because it meant either she was extraordinarily observant. Or she possessed those insights only when it came to him.

He put the cup down on a nearby counter, a prop in the game that had become his life.

Hell, he wasn't even sure what he was doing here. Just that he couldn't stand the thought of being any-where else at that moment. His apartment was quiet. Too quiet. The bar too noisy. His bottle of Jack Daniel's unappealing.

He felt a bit like Goldilocks in the story of the Three Bears. And right now Lizzie was his just right bowl of porridge…not to mention her bed.

"Do you want to come in?" she asked.

"If I'm not interrupting."

"To the contrary. You're probably saving me from an hour wasted watching a television show that doesn't interest me." She turned. "Would you like some coffee or something to drink? Bourbon or whiskey?"

He shook his head, following as she led him into the family room.

He'd viewed the room from the outside in, but it looked different from this vantage point, the recessed lighting and knickknacks and bookshelves giving it a cozy feel. Lizzie picked up the remote and shut off the television.

"Please, sit down."

He did. And if she found it intriguing that he chose the spot he usually saw her sitting in, pushing the lap blanket to the side, she didn't say anything. Instead she sat on the other side of the same couch, tucking one of her legs under her as she faced him.

"Do you want to talk about it?" she asked.

He found himself peering at her closely again. "Talk about what?"

"About what put that crease between your brows."

He gave a halfhearted grin. Maybe this hadn't been such a good idea. He'd come here to forget what had happened, not dwell on it.

"I'd just as soon not talk about it."

She looked at him for a long moment and then nodded. "That's fine." She settled in a little more comfortably against the cushions. "We can just sit here and say nothing if you want. I've had a bit of a...trying day myself. And right now, with you here, I feel quiet."

He raised a brow. "Quiet?"

"Mmm. It's a good thing. About a half hour ago I was ready to jump out of my skin."

He couldn't imagine what could have shaken what he guessed were nerves of steel. But he didn't ask, either. Normally, he didn't have to. He found that others talked about what they wanted to regardless of whether you wanted to hear it or not.

Which made Lizzie's silence all the more resounding.

"Do you mind?" he asked, gesturing toward her stereo system.

"Go ahead."

He got up and crossed to crouch in front of the expensive system. It took a moment to find the power button, and instantly the room was filled with the sound of Nina Simone. Her choice of music surprised him.

In the months that he'd lived there, he'd formed his own opinions about her and her likes and dislikes. He would have guessed her more the classical type. Bach. Or maybe Schumann. But not the blues.

He glanced over at her DVD collection, finding some interesting action films, and then got up to walk to her bookshelf. She had Jules Verne, Asimov and Wells. There was even a section on what looked like contemporary romantic novels.

Definitely not what he'd expected.

Which meant there was far more to the driven attorney than he'd thought.

He picked up a five-by-seven frame of her with a guy and a girl who had the same blond hair and similar features. Her siblings?

"So?" she said softly.

He turned to see her watching him as he put the frame back. "So what?"

"So what do you make of me?"

He gave her a lopsided smile. "That you're more complex than I thought."

"Is that good or bad?"

"Neither. It just is."

She smiled and tilted her chin into her chest, causing her golden blond hair to fall over her face. The flames in the grate seemed to light it on fire and gave her an almost ethereally sexy look. "Good answer."

He moved to stand next to her side of the couch. "I

get the impression that you like to classify everything neatly into either the good or bad column."

She looked up at him.

"Where do I fall?" he asked.

She languidly reached out and hooked her index finger into one of the belt loops on his jeans. "Both."

"Oh?"

He watched the pupils enlarge in her blue eyes. "Mmm."

Her hum was husky, vibrating.

"Bad because I shouldn't have done…shouldn't be doing what I'm doing."

Her long, manicured fingers slid from the waist of his jeans to cup his arousal beneath his closed fly. "And good because?"

She licked her lips. "Good because it seems to be just what I need right now."

He caught her hand against his fly, pressing it more insistently against him, absorbing the warmth of her that seeped through his veins as effectively as any whiskey.

"Tell me, Lizzie," he murmured, tipping her chin up with his other hand. "Is there any room for gray in your life?"

She blinked, staring at him from under the fringe of her dark lashes. "None."

She shifted her hand so that her fingertips dipped inside the waist of his jeans, wedging between the heavy material and his skin. The movement, combined with her boldness, made him rock hard.

He'd known many women in his life. Some shy and

submissive. Others brash and forceful. The ones he chose to spend time with depended more on his mood at the time he met them rather than the qualities of the women themselves. But Lizzie... Beyond her confident, icy exterior, he glimpsed something soft and vulnerable, and the contrast drew him in.

She began undoing the buttons on his jeans. He let her.

Within moments, she weighed his length in her hot palm. She shifted on the couch until she sat on the edge. The movement caught his attention in the glass of the balcony doors behind her. The recessed lights shone like a spotlight on her so that her hair glowed, while he stood in shadow.

It was surreal to be standing on this side of the window, watching their reflection, rather than on the outside looking in.

She slid her mouth over the head of his erection. He closed his eyes and clenched his teeth together, sweet sensation pooling in his balls.

Lizzie curved her fingers around the base of him and held him straight as she took more of him in, swirling her tongue around his shaft then backing away before going down on him again.

Gauge slowly touched her hair, fingering the soft strands. There were few things more beautiful than a hot woman who knew how to please a man. Knew how to please *him*.

He reached behind her, tugging on her sweater until she broke contact and allowed him to strip it from her. Her back was long and graceful, appearing ghostly white in the glass. He smoothed his palms down her shoulders and unhooked her bra, watching as she shook it off, the orbs of her breasts swaying tantalizingly.

Gauge groaned as she once again took him into her mouth and increased suction, his hips bucking involuntarily.

He pushed her hair back from her face so he could view her attentions directly, mesmerized by the fit of her lips, the flicks of her tongue, the grip of her hand…a hand that squeezed him and then curved down to cup his balls.

He stiffened in preparation for orgasm, hoping she wouldn't pull away too soon. Instead, she sucked until he was sure he'd filled her mouth, and then moved his shaft to her breasts, squeezing the full mounds of flesh together to sandwich him there, prolonging his climax until he was afraid he'd emptied himself….

7

LIZZIE RAN her tongue along the head of Gauge's erection, finding that he was surprisingly still hard. His fingers were entwined in her hair, not quite pulling, not quite caressing. They shifted from her head to her shoulders, where he coaxed her to rise from the couch.

She stood quietly facing him, the taste of him still ripe in her mouth. He seemed to be inordinately interested in her lips, his gaze lingering there even as he unfastened the catch on her slacks and pushed the fabric down over her hips along with her panties, skimming his fingers across her bare bottom, where they dipped into the shallow crevice before moving up her back. She shivered. Not from the cold but from the intensity of his expression, combined with his knowing touch.

Then he did something she would never have expected, given his words of the previous evening: he kissed her.

Lizzie caught her breath at the first feathery pass of his lips against hers. She was a little more prepared when he returned, kissing him back.

There was an art to kissing. A finesse that she found most men either chose to ignore or didn't take the time to master, but if done right, was almost enough to bring a woman to climax without touching her anywhere else.

Gauge's kiss was a masterpiece.

She made quick work of stripping him of the rest of his clothes and then melted into his embrace, satisfied to be making out with him. Enjoying the tangling of his tongue with hers. His mint-fresh breath mingling with hers. He slid his right hand from her back to her front, gently cupping her breast. He caught her nipple between his thumb and index finger, rolling the tight, sensitive tip. She moaned, curving her own hands down over his backside, reveling in the muscled length of him as she pressed her stomach against his thick erection...aching to feel him somewhere else.

Lizzie realized she had closed her eyes and slightly opened them again, wanting to verify that she was, indeed, standing completely naked in her family room, curtains wide-open, kissing an equally nude Gauge. He seemed to sense that she was watching him and his eyes opened slightly, as well. She read vague surprise in their green depths.

He switched his attention from her mouth to her neck and shoulder.

Lizzie couldn't help thinking that his movement wasn't generated by a sudden desire to taste her skin, and she felt a moment of loss. She tried to guide his mouth back to hers, but he resisted, distracting her instantly by plunging his fingers into her damp channel from behind, parting her to the cool air.

He grasped her hips and turned her. It was only then that she became aware that they were fully reflected in the balcony doors. She readily bent over, arching her back so her bottom thrust up toward him in open invitation. He gamely responded by sheathing himself with a condom he took from the back pocket of his jeans where they lay on the floor.

Lizzie placed her hands on the couch back, bracing herself for his breach. Instead, he used his hand to caress her with his hard-on, moving the head along her damp opening and back again, then sandwiching himself between the folds of her swollen flesh and pressing the head against her clit.

She gasped, pure, wanton need pulsing through her veins. She hungered for him to fill her, and the longer he delayed the more she wanted him.

She reached between her legs and took his thick, heavy length in her palm, restlessly positioning him against her portal and bearing down on him even as he continued to stand still. Inch by inch, she slid back, her breasts seeming to throb along with the rest of her.

Lizzie caught his gaze in the glass as he watched their coupling as openly as she did. She restlessly licked her lips. He finally grasped her hips, his fingers imprinting her skin as he thrust into her.

She moaned, filled beyond expectation with hard, hot man and sweet, erotic desire.

He thrust again as she clutched the couch and braced

herself for his deep strokes. She watched her breasts shudder as flesh slapped against flesh. Felt his balls sway against her with each meeting. She'd never witnessed herself in such a carnal state and was mesmerized by their reflection. By the fullness of her breasts, the pertness of her ass, the provocative bowing of her mouth. The intense expression on Gauge's face, the rippling of his abs, the easy way he held himself as if taking her from behind in her family room was what he was born to do.

She reached between her legs again, finding the sensitive sac and fondling it. Gauge made a sound deep in his throat, the intensity of his thrusts increasing. When he stiffened in climax, deep within her, she tumbled happily and wantonly right after him....

"So WHO HE IS?" Tabby asked her the following day.

Lizzie stared at her friend across the cafeteria-style table. They were supposed to meet at a restaurant for lunch, but Tabby had talked her into going to the mall instead, where they could combine two tasks in one: Christmas shopping and a quick meal. So they sat in the food court, purchases propped on the chairs on either side of them, trays on the table. Lizzie had gone with a calzone, while Tabby opted for a garden salad.

"Who's who?" she asked, taking a sip of her diet soda and watching a couple pass by arm in arm.

Tabby waved her hand and stabbed at her salad with her plastic fork. "You're eating a calzone."

Lizzie raised her brows. "I'm not following you."

"We both eat salads at lunch…unless one of us has had some hot, sweaty sex the night before."

Lizzie threw her head back and laughed. "Maybe I just felt like a calzone."

"Yeah, and I'm Mother Teresa."

Lizzie concentrated on eating as she looked at her watch. She was already running late. She wanted to get in at least a half hour of note reading before this afternoon's meeting.

But that's not really where her mind was. Instead, Tabby's question had made her remember last night and her sexy time with Gauge.

He'd kissed her. Just the once. And he'd gone out of his way to keep from kissing her again. But she hadn't minded because she'd been too occupied with other things to notice much.

Tabitha was right. She'd chosen the calzone because she could.

"So what gives?"

Lizzie gave an exaggerated sigh. "Nothing," she insisted.

And, all things considered, she was being honest, wasn't she? There was nothing going on. Nothing fit to mention, anyway. While she and Gauge had had great sex—twice—there was nothing beyond that, and there was absolutely no guarantee that it would happen again, so why introduce the subject? Especially since she was sure to hear "So how's that sexy musician you're screwing?" for weeks afterward.

"Anyway," she said, wiping a smear of tomato from

the heel of her hand. "Don't even mention the word *sex* to me. Not after what I saw in my old bedroom at my parents' place."

Now that episode she had no problem telling Tabby about. Her friend had already heard the majority of the Gilbred kids' stories of their parents' shenanigans while they were growing up. This made a nice little addition to the collection.

"Do you think they're reconciling?" Tabby asked.

Lizzie knew that her friend's own parents had divorced long ago and that they didn't even acknowledge the other's existence, much less show any signs of possible reconciliation. Tabitha had told her she'd never been so happy as on her graduation day when she wouldn't have to rely on her mother or father financially again. She'd felt liberated from their lingering bitterness. She now joked that her only future worries were the day of her wedding—if she married—and any possible events surrounding children she might have. Otherwise, she was as free as a bird, planning out holidays way in advance just so everyone knew what she was doing when. She'd long since become a pro at dodging leading questions like "What did your father give you?" or "Does your mother have her talons into any new men?"

That was precisely the reason Lizzie was worried about her own parents' marriage. If their acrimonious separation was any indication, then life for the Gilbred offspring would be hell on earth from here on out.

"I don't know," she replied honestly. "I haven't

talked to my mother yet." And, boy, she was dreading the moment.

"I hope they are. I wouldn't wish that part of my life on anybody." Tabby chewed on a bite of salad. "One of the reasons I made friends with you in college was because I wanted to adopt your family."

"More like my family adopted you."

Tabby's smile of gratitude warmed Lizzie.

When Lizzie looked at her watch this time, she did so with genuine concern. "God, I'm so late."

"Yes, but just think what Christmas shopping you got done."

"Considering that I don't even know if there will be a Christmas," Lizzie said, "I'm not so sure how smart that was."

What she *was* sure about was that thinking of Gauge and wondering what he might like for Christmas was a dumb idea.

8

GAUGE SAT on the bandstand, tuning his guitar without the aid of the amp. He was early. The rest of the band wasn't due to arrive for another hour.

But he wasn't there because he wanted to win any brownie points. He'd come because Kevin had called and asked him to.

He ran his fingers along the frets, practicing one of the songs in the first set of the night—Bob Seger's "Night Moves," which was always a hit with the Michigan natives. There were a few people in the pub, mostly lingering over dinner, and no one save for a woman in the far booth and one of the waitresses was paying any attention to him.

He put the guitar pick between his teeth and ran his hand through his hair, the strands still damp from the snow that had been falling as he walked from his parked car to the pub. It was going to be a cold, nasty night. The type of night that should keep people indoors until the storm passed. But it was also Friday, and no matter the weather, most people were determined to get out and celebrate the end of another workweek.

Yes, he knew what that was like. Although his first attempt at an ordinary life had happened so long ago it was now little more than a bad memory. And seeing as it had lasted only six months, well, it was easy to understand why he didn't think about it often.

What he did remember was the girl responsible for the one-eighty he'd tried to make.

He took the pick out of his mouth and played a song from those days. A song he refused to play for entertainment purposes, although it was probably the one he played best.

Over the years he'd learned that he had at least two half brothers and a half sister out there somewhere. Love children created by his father with different women during one- or two-night stands. Gauge had never considered trying to bond with any of his half siblings. He figured one reason might be that they were spread out across the country, conceived during travel gigs that had taken him and his father as far north as British Columbia and as far south as Key West. But the truth was, he had never felt a desire to get to know any of them. And apparently none of them had any desire to meet him, either. Maybe because he was his father's first illegitimate son, he'd gotten the attention that none of them would.

It was difficult to ignore one child. Easier to ignore four.

He recalled a time when one of his half brothers had confronted them at a bar they were playing in Santa Fe. Gauge had been maybe fifteen at the time, old enough to play at the bar, but not old enough to drink at it. The kid, Gorge, had been about twelve, thirteen, and was a good-looking kid of obviously mixed heritage. At first, Gauge thought Gorge might sucker punch Thomas Gauge. And he'd been fully prepared to let him do it. He figured the kid deserved at least that. If not more.

But his father had walked off with the troubled teen and the pair had talked in the gravel parking lot for about a half hour. Gauge had stood right outside the door during the unexpected break from playing and smoked a cigarette, watching the two men from a distance. Then his father had taken some money from his back pocket, pressed it into the kid's hand and given him an awkward hug.

Gauge had waited for his father to explain. If not then, at some point. But he never did. He'd merely slapped Gauge on the shoulder as he passed him on his way back inside the bar—alone—and said, "Come on. We've got to do what we were paid to do."

"Gauge."

He hadn't realized he'd closed his eyes until he heard the waitress's voice.

He automatically twirled the guitar and positioned it in its stand, pretending that her interruption had not mattered. But it had. He didn't know what was responsible for his visit to the long-ago past, but he was positive that it was something he didn't want to think about.

"Kevin's at the bar asking for you," Debbie said, poking a thumb over her shoulder.

Gauge leaned over to see around her. Sure enough, Kevin sat on one of the stools with his back to Gauge, pretending to be relaxed even though it was obvious he was anything but.

Sorry sap.

Gauge rose from his playing chair and slid the pick into his jeans pocket, then stepped from the slightly raised stage.

He headed over to the bar, slanting his old friend a glance while he placed his order. "Hey, Charlie, slide one of those cold drafts my way."

"Sure thing, Gauge."

If he'd thought Kevin was rigid before, he now figured his friend's spine might snap in two. He couldn't help but be amused, even though there wasn't anything remotely funny about their situation.

Charlie put a glass in front of him and he gestured toward Kevin. "You sure you don't want something stronger than beer? Looks like you could use it."

His friend's expression told him he needed something else that had nothing to do with alcohol and everything to do with evening the score.

Kevin reached into his brown suede jacket and took out an envelope. Gauge frowned as Kevin put it on the bar and slid it toward him. "Your monthly take."

The money owed him for his third share of BMC. He folded the envelope three times and slid it into his back pocket without looking at it.

"Don't you want to see how much it is?" Kevin asked.

"No."

"We had a good month what with Christmas shopping and everything. You should be pleased."

He wasn't.

In fact, he had yet to cash a single one of the monthly checks that Kevin and Nina had given him. They sat in a kitchen drawer at his apartment, all but the first envelope unopened.

Kevin stared straight ahead and sipped his beer. Which reminded Gauge of the reason the bar was the favorite place of loners. You could sit all night and drink and not have to look at or talk to anyone if you didn't want to.

"That's why you asked me to meet you here? To give me the check?"

A pause, and then, "Among other things."

Gauge rested his forearms on the counter. "Plan on getting to the point anytime soon?"

That got an irritated rise out of Kevin.

"Look, we could pretend for forever and a day that what happened ten months ago didn't happen, man," Gauge said, surprised to find he was growing agitated. Damn it, if you had a problem, you put it out there. It was as simple as that. He didn't like the hemming and hawing that so many people indulged in.

He didn't like the beating around the bush that Kevin was known for.

He laughed without humor. "You know, it's that silent brooding of yours that got us all into trouble in the first place."

Kevin swiveled toward him so fast Gauge nearly put his arm out to ward off an impending blow. He knew that he deserved whatever was coming his way and almost hoped that his friend would finally unleash his anger on him the way he apparently wanted to.

But, as usual, Kevin kept a tight rein on his emotions. "Are you saying I'm to blame for your sleeping with my wife?"

"She wasn't your wife then."

"No, but you knew how I felt about her, damn it. And you still slept with her."

He'd heard the words before. And nothing had changed. And nothing would unless he forced it. He looked carefully, purposely at his friend and said, "Actually, I don't think you can call what Nina and I did in the back of the music center as sleeping. What do you think?"

Kevin clenched his jaw so tightly, Gauge swore he could almost hear his friend's teeth grinding. "I think I rue the day you ever came to this town."

They stared at each other for a long moment, then Gauge sighed and faced the front of the bar again, resting his boot heel against the brass footrest.

He recalled a time when that hadn't been the case. When he'd been welcome in this town, not only as the owner of the music center, but as Kevin's friend. His best friend.

And as much as it pained him to say it, it bothered him that he no longer held that title.

In fact, it was the sole reason he'd come back to town. To try to repair burned bridges. And while it was taking far longer than he would have expected, he didn't think it was a lost cause. Not yet.

Truth was, he was searching for something more meaningful than this ceaseless wandering from place to place, bed to bed.

And he'd gotten a glimpse of it during his three-year friendship with Kevin and Nina.

He looked to find his friend staring straight ahead, as well. If only Gauge didn't suspect that any forward progress depended on repairing things between them.

He cleared his throat. "It's probably not a very good idea to marry someone you don't trust. They say trust is the bedrock of any good relationship." He shook his head. "If you don't trust Nina now…"

Gauge purposely left his words hanging. He knew he was essentially egging on a grizzly bear by taunting Kevin. But beyond offering himself up as bait, he didn't know how else the two of them were going to move beyond this bar counter, much less beyond what had happened between the three of them ten months ago.

Kevin stared at him. "I trust my wife with my life."

"But do you trust her beyond your bed?"

Finally, Kevin reacted in a way that went beyond words. He got up from the stool so fast he nearly knocked it over and grabbed the front of Gauge's shirt, hauling him up. "Goddamn it, Gauge, you're not going to be happy until I offer to fight you, are you?"

Gauge looked down to emphasize their positions. "If that's the case, it looks like I'm about to get what I want."

Kevin's breathing was hard as he considered his options.

Finally, he released Gauge and gave him a bit of a

shove. "No. No matter how much I'd love to bury my fist in your smug face, I'm not going to do it. I'm not going to let myself be manipulated into communicating in the only way you apparently know how, through sarcasm and physical force." He picked up his coat from a neighboring stool and shrugged into it, keeping his gaze locked on Gauge's. He pointed a finger at Gauge, nearly poking his chest. "I wouldn't even be here if not for Nina. She has some romanticized idea about the three of us becoming friends again. Says you need us." He shook his head. "And before you can make another smart-ass remark, let me tell you this—I'd do anything for my wife. Anything. But if we're going to get through this, we're going to do it my way, not yours. I will not be badgered into a physical fight."

He peeled off a few bills and laid them on the bar.

"Oh, and one more thing," he said, turning toward Gauge. "It's not my wife I don't trust—it's you. And until—if—I can, then we have nothing to say to each other."

Gauge sat back on the stool and watched his friend go.

There had been few men in his life that had made him proud. And, he realized, Kevin was one of them.

While he teased him for his quiet ways, Gauge had always known that underneath his polite exterior lay cold steel. Kevin was more than bookishly smart, he was wise.

And no matter how angry he was, he'd never give himself over to the dark side that Gauge had known for so much of his life.

He absently sipped his beer, still staring at the closed door.

"What was that about?" Charlie asked, taking Kevin's abandoned mug and wiping the bar.

Gauge shook his head. "Nothing."

But that wasn't true, was it? Because it was about everything. At least everything that had once been important to him.

And still was.

The question was, how did you regain trust once you lost it? And was it even possible to do?

He didn't know.

What he did know was that he wasn't leaving town until he figured it out.

9

LIZZIE PUT the delicate angel on top of the small tree she'd set up next to the fireplace in the family room and then sat back on her heels, considering her handiwork. She hadn't planned to decorate her place for Christmas beyond having a professional hang the plain white lights on the front of the house along with a large wreath, as was the tradition in the neighborhood. But she'd knocked off from the firm early and found herself stopping to pick out a tree from a lot that had been temporarily rented for the season and stocked with all sorts of different varieties of evergreens. She'd purposely chosen a small, potted pine that she would replant in the backyard after New Year's.

She glanced toward the window at the snow falling, lightening the darkness. Spring seemed so far off just then.

She got up and plugged the lights in, standing back and smiling as the multicolored string began dancing and blinking.

She'd always loved the holidays. Her parents had made sure to make the days between Thanksgiving and New Year's as magical as possible for their three kids. She remembered hunting through a tree farm in the snow with their father, animatedly trying to decide which tree would grace their home that year. Sleigh rides through the snow-covered fields. Heaping mugs of hot chocolate piled with marshmallows. And always, always, there were Christmas carols playing in the background. Whether they were decorating cookies with their mother in the kitchen, or wrapping presents or getting ready to head out to church in their new clothes on Sunday, the carols seemed to set the mood.

Lizzie smiled now, listening to the Ella Fitzgerald Christmas CD she'd put on as she positioned one of the five poinsettias she'd bought around the fireplace. Of course, her memory was probably distorting things a bit. It was impossible that the holidays had been all that perfect. There had been bruised knees during ice skating mishaps, tears after sledding accidents, and on more than one occasion, the three Gilbred siblings had happened upon their parents demonstrating their own kind of Christmas cheer by getting it on wherever and whenever they could. It seemed that Bonnie and Clyde never failed in their ability to shock their three children.

And now wasn't any different. Only the shocks they were delivering went well beyond passionate little quickies.

Lizzie moved to the couch and considered the Christmas cards she'd bought and laid out, along with a pad and her laptop, which held her electronic address book. Like the decorating, she hadn't planned on sending out cards, but as soon as she'd given in to one thing, she'd found herself going the whole nine yards.

Well, she'd also been spurred on by her sister Annie's frantic call to go to a specialty store near the law firm to pick up a particular type of boxed cards because she'd run out. Annie always sent everyone the same card because, as she explained, what if someone thought that somebody else's card was better?

Besides, it kept things simpler that way and basically guaranteed that the same cards wouldn't be sent out the following year.

There was a certain logic to her sister's way of doing things, Lizzie thought, however boring.

While she was at the store she'd chosen individual cards for herself, some with music, some sentimental, others with a racy humor that would make Santa drop his jaw in shock.

"So what do you think?" her sister had asked her when she'd dropped the requested cards off at what Lizzie called the House of Chaos. "Do you think we're going to have Christmas at the parents' this year? Or should we maybe do it here?"

Lizzie had looked down at a cookie-crumb-covered Mason in her arms, drooling on her two-hundred-dollar sweater, then eyed three-year-old Jasmine's race through the living room on her tricycle. Any direct route in the house was impeded by scattered toys and a stray pet or two.

"Absolutely not," she said.

Lizzie was going to insist that they all gather at the

Gilbred family home and make the holidays happen, come hell or high water. She didn't care if her mother poisoned the turkey or if her father locked himself up in his study. Come Christmas morning, that's where she planned to be and she told Annie that she and their brother, Jesse, should have the same plan.

While Annie had looked dubious, Lizzie could see the wheels begin to turn in her head. Probably she was already thinking about going over to decorate the house like her mother used to and was planning the menu for Christmas dinner. So be it. As long as she did it in the house where they'd all grown up, Lizzie could eat her sister's idea of a holiday dinner, which would likely be a recipe out of one of her hundred cookbooks with *l'orange* something or other.

In the midst of her thoughts she realized she'd relaxed into her sofa with a cup of hot chocolate that was more lukewarm and was staring out the window.

It didn't take a rocket scientist to know what she was looking for. Or, more specifically, who.

But Gauge wasn't in his apartment. It was Friday night and he was playing down at the pub.

The image of him strumming his guitar on a bandstand made her hot.

But even if he had been home, there was no guarantee that they would be spending the night together. As he'd so refreshingly pointed out during their first night together, their relationship was all about sex. Nothing more. Nothing less.

And if her mind kept wandering back to their long,

leisurely kiss from the night before…well, that was because it had been so good. Nothing more. Nothing less.

At any rate, that morning while checking her cell-phone messages, she'd come across Jerry's text good-bye. And had taken great pleasure in pressing the delete button.

Jerry…

Was it a bad thing that she hadn't really thought about him the past couple of days? After all, she'd thought the guy was the one. Not just now, but six years ago. Was it natural for her to have moved on so quickly after his departure? Or was she practicing some sort of avoidance therapy by not dealing with whatever deeper emotions were connected to him and their breakup?

She sipped her drink and rolled the thought around in her head as Ella sung a swinging version of "Joy to the World." But the more she tried to concentrate, the clearer the memory of last night with Gauge became.

She checked her watch. After ten. Surely it wasn't too late to drive down to the pub and catch him playing with the band. She looked out the window at the accumulating snow. Three additional inches must have fallen since she got home from work.

Lizzie chewed on her bottom lip. If she did see him tonight, it would be three times in a row.

Was she replacing one obsession with another?

Not that she thought there could ever be anything serious between her and the sexy musician. They were too different for that.

Then again, she and Jerry had shared almost a scary

number of things in common, and they hadn't been able to make it work.

"God, what are you thinking about?" she said under her breath, getting up from the couch and carrying her nearly empty cup into the kitchen. She rinsed it out and placed it in the dishwasher then stood for long minutes at the sink, listening to the silence of the house around her, which was even more pronounced because of the softly falling show outside.

Funny, she'd never really realized how quiet it was until that moment. Considering she'd lived there for half a year, that was saying something.

And here she'd thought Jerry's leaving wasn't bothering her in the least.

She sat back down in the family room, picked up the remote to lower the volume on the CD and then switched on the television to see what she could find to distract her for one blasted night. *It's a Wonderful Life* popped on.

She immediately turned the channel until she found an action flick. *Die Hard*. Yes. That should do the trick….

THE FOLLOWING DAY at lunch, Lizzie sat across from her mother, trying not to notice how…happy she looked.

When she'd finally spoken to her mother, it was only to arrange the Saturday-morning meeting. She hadn't mentioned the other night at the house. And neither had her mother. And that was fine with Lizzie. She'd rather try to forget the scene than further entrench it in her memory.

And now that her mother sat opposite her at a booth in the Greek restaurant Dimitri's in Sylvania, not too far from the law firm, where Lizzie had put in a morning of work, she wondered if it had been a good idea to meet so soon after their last encounter.

"Mmm, everything looks so good," Bonnie said, reading the menu. "You've been here before?"

"What? Oh, yes. I come often enough."

She squinted at her mother, trying to pinpoint a reason for the improvement in her appearance. A reason that didn't have anything to do with her indulging in kinky sex with her father in Lizzie's childhood bed.

"Are you going to have time to fit in a bit of shopping after lunch?" her mother asked, once they'd placed their drink orders with the friendly waitress who was one of the owner's two daughters.

"Depends."

"On what?"

On whether or not the meal goes well, Lizzie thought. "On whether I get a return call from one of the clients I was supposed to meet this morning. Why?"

Bonnie shrugged. "I don't know. I figured if we were going to do a fair amount of walking at the mall today, then I could indulge a little now. But if we're not going to, then I should keep it light."

That was it. The difference. Her mother had lost weight.

Not that she'd needed to. While Bonnie Gilbred had always been a little on the round side, she'd never really been overweight. But now that she seemed to have shed at least ten pounds, she looked almost Lizzie's age.

Lizzie frowned. Okay, maybe not her age. But certainly younger than she had looked before, which was about five years older than she was.

Lizzie rubbed her forehead, her thoughts making no sense even to herself.

"I'll just keep it light anyway," her mother said.

"Have you changed your hairstyle?" Lizzie asked.

Bonnie's hand went to her hair. "Why yes. I decided to get some of those fancy highlights put in, you know, like all you kids get nowadays." She made a face. "Your father always liked my hair dark, but now that we're not going to be married anymore, I figure it's *my* hair and I can do anything I damn well please with it." She gave a secret smile. "But between you and me, I think he liked it."

Lizzie held up her hand. "You can stop right there, thank you very much."

"Why? What's wrong?" Lizzie didn't say anything and her mother gazed down at the table. "Oh. This is about the S and M bit you walked in on the other night. I'm sorry, honey. I would have preferred you not to have seen that."

S and M? What did her mother know about S and M? Stupid question.

"It's not that, really," Lizzie said. "Well, yes it is." She leveled a stare at her mother. If they were going to talk about this, then she might as well be honest. "It was my bed."

She didn't know what she expected. A guilty expression. An apology. Instead, the elder Gilbred said, "It was the only bed in the house with four posts."

Lizzie's mouth gaped open. "Mother!"

"What? It's true."

"The bed is…was…mine."

Finally, it seemed to dawn on Bonnie why her daughter was so upset. And rather than being compassionate, she gave an eye roll to rival all eye rolls. "Oh, for god's sake, Lizzie, it's just a bed. A frame with two mattresses on it."

"It was my bed. My initials are carved in one of the bedposts."

"Yes, I was meaning to ask you when you did that. It's going to affect resale value, you know."

Lizzie's mouth worked around a response…only it refused to come. "What?" she fairly croaked.

"Well, you didn't think we were going to keep it forever, did you? Especially the way things stand. With your father and me getting a divorce, we're going to have to sell everything, divide up the money and move on with our lives…" She trailed off. "Although Clyde's saying he'd rather work out a different arrangement. Something like he buys out my half of the house and I pay him rent."

"Rent?" Lizzie repeated. How could her mother talk about these matters with such ease, as if they were as unimportant as the shape of the water glasses on the table? "You haven't worked for years. How are you going to pay rent?"

"There will be the money I get in the settlement," she said. "And then there's the job interview I have in January."

"What job interview?"

"With a fancy airline." She shifted and grinned. "I want to be a flight attendant."

Lizzie nearly spit out the water she'd just put in her mouth. "A what?"

Bonnie waved her hand. "Don't look so shocked. I was a great waitress in my day. And one of my old high school friends just got a job doing the same thing in California. The airlines are looking for us older girls with more life experience."

"And probably less pension requirements."

"Okay, fine. They don't pay as much as they used to, but seeing I've wanted to do this since I was a kid, well, I'd pay them for the experience."

Her mother. The flight attendant.

Someone wake her up from this nightmare.

Bonnie opened her mouth again and Lizzie held up her hand. "Please. That's enough for one day. What's say we just order and enjoy our meal, all right?" She re-arranged the salt and pepper shakers, something, anything so she wouldn't have to look at her mother's crestfallen expression. "Have you talked to Annie today?"

Thankfully, Bonnie was just as happy to talk about her pregnant daughter as she was about the other areas of her life. Lizzie encouraged her as she reached for a bottle of extra-strength pain reliever in her purse.

10

SATURDAY NIGHT, Lizzie met Tabby for a late dinner. But rather than heading to a movie they were both ambivalent about seeing, Lizzie suggested they go somewhere else.

"A bar?" Tabitha said to her as she held aloft the last nacho oozing with cheese. She put it down and reached for a napkin. "Are you suggesting we, gasp, go to a meat market?"

Lizzie slowly sipped her coffee, hiding her smile. "It's not anything as nefarious as that. The place I'm thinking about is a pub, not a full-out bar."

"Meaning that they serve frozen chicken nuggets with the beer."

"Or nachos," she said, indicating the congealed mixture on the plate that had been on their table since their appetizers were served. Tabby had refused to allow the waiter to take it because she intended to eat every last one if it killed her.

"Ha-ha. You're a real hoot, Liz." Tabby sat back in the booth. "God, I wish you had said something before I ordered. I feel like I've put on five pounds in the past hour."

"That's because you probably have."

Tabby grimaced. "That's what Mondays are for. To fast to make up for Saturdays."

"You mean, Mondays, Tuesdays and Wednesdays."

"Yeah, what is it with that, anyway? Is it just me, or are the days gone when you could cut back one day and lose five pounds?"

"Definitely not just you. Which is why I ordered the black-bean soup."

Tabby waggled her finger at Lizzie. "No, you ordered the black-bean soup because you knew you were going to suggest going out. Only, you don't have to worry about any temporary tummy bulges showing on that sleek physique of yours."

"We don't have to go if you don't want to."

"Aha!"

"Aha what?"

"You knew I wouldn't be able to resist going to a bar with you. Now you'll have room for drinks, and I—" She sat back in the booth and groaned again. "God, I feel like a stuffed turkey."

"Yeah, well, you look great."

Tabby raised a skeptical brow. "Here I was planning on going light at the movies, you know, choosing a box of Raisinets over the Goobers and popcorn with extra butter, and all along you were saving room for apple martinis."

"I already said that we don't have to go."

"Of course we have to go. What, and pass up the opportunity for me to see this guy you've been sleeping with?" She raised her hand, ignoring Lizzie's gasp. "Check, please. Oh, and bring one of those take-out cartons, will you?"

Gauge wasn't sure how he knew the moment Lizzie entered, but he did. He rarely if ever watched the door, but tonight his gaze had gone to it the minute it opened and she walked inside with a dark-haired girlfriend. Just seeing her shrug out of her coat as the two took a table that had emptied in the middle of the room made it seem suddenly hot inside the bar. Not that she was wearing anything overtly sexy. That wasn't Lizzie's style. But knowing how very hot she was under that conservative clothing filled his mind with all sorts of erotic, welcome images.

The song ended and the group of young women who were already half in the bag near the front of the stage whistled and hooted and hollered. They'd just started the set or else he'd have asked the lead singer to break. As it was, he had to get through another hour of playing before he could think about making his way to Lizzie's table.

He only hoped she stayed long enough.

Last night, the echo from the amplifiers ringing in his head, he'd lain awake wondering if four in the morning was too late to go knocking on Lizzie's door. Of course, it had been. Her house had been dark when he'd returned home.

So he lay for a long time going over everything in his head. His conversation with Kevin. The night at the bar. Lizzie sleeping alone in her bed across the driveway. The fact that with anyone else, he wouldn't have thought twice before knocking on her door.

So why hadn't he gone over to Lizzie's?

He looked at her now as she took a long sip from a Guinness, returning his gaze as she did so. Damn, the woman was beautiful. But so were at least five other females in the joint that night. Why, then, did he feel like the air was being forced from his body when he looked at her?

His father had told him once that a man was lucky if he found love, real love, at least once in his life. And given his own experiences, Gauge was beginning to fear that was true. Oh, there was the temporary thrill of the hunt. The rush of sex with a stranger. But both were almost always followed by the desire to chase the same person from your bed the next morning with absolutely no interest in finding out what they liked for breakfast.

Then there was the fact that he *had* found love. With a woman who was married to his best friend.

Was it greedy to want another go at it? Was it even possible that he could be given the chance? Or would what he was feeling for Lizzie pass when he awakened one morning to find that she wasn't beautiful at all, but painfully normal? And that it wasn't enough for him anymore?

The lead singer acknowledged his playing along with the other band members and the patrons ignited in applause and cheers. He gave a thank-you run, but the only person that mattered was Lizzie. And she was standing and giving a wolf whistle.

"WELL, OKAY THEN. Mystery solved," Tabby said after Lizzie sat back down.

Lizzie slanted her friend a look, only to find her grinning.

Tabby held up her hands. "Hey, he's the hottest guy in the bar and he's a musician. What's not to like about that?"

She took a long pull of her Guinness.

"What?"

Lizzie shook her head. "I'm waiting for the rest."

"Rest? There is no rest." Tabby stuck her finger into her apple martini and sucked on the tip.

The band segued into the next song and Lizzie felt the incredible urge to dance. An urge she battled back because she knew her friend wasn't done. Tabby was never done. And Lizzie felt she needed to hear whatever she had to say.

"Just tell me the sex is great."

"The sex is mind blowing."

"Great. Great would have covered it. Mind blowing?" Tabby sat back and made a face. "It's official. I hate you."

Lizzie smiled. She'd never been officially hated before.

She began to rise and pull her friend up to go dance on the narrow floor in front of the band. Tabby caught her arm.

Uh-oh. She was afraid this was the "real rest" she'd been waiting for.

"You do know that it's temporary, though, right? I mean, I don't know anyone who goes on to marry one of these guys."

Lizzie laughed and yanked on her hand. "Of course I know it's temporary," she said. "Let's dance."

"Dance? We don't dance. Oh!" She stumbled to her feet and had to fight to keep balanced. "Okay, so we're dancing…."

THREE HOURS LATER, Gauge left the pub and made his way home. Lizzie and her friend had left some time before. Which had surprised him. He had hoped she would stay. Or at least made arrangements to meet up with him either at his place or hers.

Instead, she'd given him a brief wave from across the room and she and her friend had left.

He'd been disappointed, but not entirely surprised. When she'd introduced him to her friend, Tabitha, she hadn't said anything about his renting the apartment above her garage. So probably she'd left to make it look like they weren't returning to the same place.

He parked his car at the curb and walked through the snow that had accumulated on the driveway toward the back of the house, the tire tracks left by her car when she'd come home almost covered. He stopped short of the garage and turned toward Lizzie's place. Not a single window was lit.

He squinted against the light snowflakes that blew into his eyes. A sign that she wasn't looking for company tonight?

If so, then he'd misread her every signal at the pub. Because every time he'd looked at her, she'd worn the sly, suggestive expression that was timeless when it came to the mating dance.

Still, it appeared she'd come home and gone to bed. Alone.

If she'd wanted him to interrupt, at the very least she might have left a candle in the window.

He absently rubbed his chin, hunkered down further into his denim jacket, and continued on toward the garage. He climbed the stairs, shaking off the snow and cold before stepping inside. It was warmer than he expected. Hadn't he lowered the thermostat before leaving? He was pretty sure he had. But maybe he was remembering yesterday.

He shrugged out of his coat and went to the refrigerator, the inside light the only thing brightening the rest of the apartment. He took out the bottle of cold water there, drank a good portion of it, then walked toward the bed. He sat down and began taking off his boots.

"I thought you'd never get home," a familiar voice whispered. "One of the perks of being the landlord—I have my own key."

He grinned as a warm hand reached from between the sheets and touched his back, tunneling under his T-shirt to make contact with his skin.

He had never been happier that his ability to read women was target on.

LIZZIE HADN'T KNOWN what Gauge might make of her waiting for him, naked in his own bed, but she'd been unable to help herself when the idea occurred to her at the pub. She supposed it was the combination of the beer she'd drunk and the heightened sense of awareness that had grown all night.

She'd wanted Gauge, and she'd wanted him now.

But now that she had him, she was in no hurry. They had all night long to satisfy the hunger that roared inside her.

"On the surprise scale, I'd say this one rates a ten," he said, kicking off his boots and pulling off his T-shirt. He stretched to lie on top of the bedding while she was underneath. He rolled her closer to him, burying his hand in her hair.

"A good surprise?"

"Mmm. A very good surprise." He folded his other hand to support his head. "It was nice to see you at the pub tonight."

Lizzie splayed her fingers against his chest and the soft, light hair there. He was cold from having been outside, but was warming quickly. He smelled of freshly fallen snow and one hundred percent hot male. "Are you sure? There seemed to be about five other girls there vying for your attention."

"Mmm." He rested his chin on top of her head when she laid her cheek against his chest. "No, they were vying for the lead guitar player. You were the only one genuinely there for me." He turned her face to look at him.

"How can you be so sure it was you I was there to see?" She smiled. "Maybe I go to the pub all the time. Maybe it was a coincidence that you play there. Maybe Tabby's a frequent visitor."

He chuckled softly. "Right."

"God, I hate that I'm so predictable."

"Honey, your being there tonight was as unpredictable as they come."

She pressed her cheek against his shoulder, enjoying being this close to him. "Tabby liked you."

"Mmm. Your friend."

"She liked you a lot."

He didn't respond immediately, then said, "Well, I suppose I should be glad I came home to find you in my bed instead of her then, shouldn't I?"

She laughed and rolled on top of him, straddling him so that her naked womanhood rested against the front of his jeans.

"Would you have been that disappointed?"

He reached up, curving his hand around her neck and urging her closer to him. He paused when she was a breath away from kissing him. "I would have been very disappointed, indeed."

11

"I WANT TO SEE YOU…"

Gauge listened to the message on his machine that must have been there since before he returned home last night. He glanced across the room at his bed, where Lizzie still lay sleeping. The white sheets were tangled and, halfway down her back, her hair spilled across his pillow like liquid sunshine.

He knew a pang of regret. He'd gotten up to use the bathroom with every intention of returning to the warm bed with Lizzie in it. But he'd seen the message button flashing and checked it just in case one of the band members had called with a change of plans.

Instead it had been Nina.

He went into the bathroom and took a quick shower and then stayed in the kitchen, which gave him privacy from the sleeping area, and went about making coffee. It was after nine on a Sunday, but he knew that Nina would be at the bookstore café already.

Nina…

He stood, waiting for the coffee to brew, his mind filling with images of another time, another woman… and the other man who loved her.

"I would never have figured you for a morning person," Lizzie's sleepy voice said from behind him.

Gauge frowned, jerked from his thoughts. "I'm not."

There was a long silence. He turned to see her leaning against the counter, a sheet wrapped around her body. Her expression was pensive.

"Are you okay?" she asked.

Damn.

He still hadn't completely figured Lizzie out. But for reasons he had yet to fully explore, she seemed tuned into him on a level he couldn't ignore.

"Yeah, I'm all right. Just got a call from an old friend, is all."

She apparently noted the honesty of the answer and came up behind him, holding him for a long moment, her soft warmth encompassing him so that he longed to turn into her and carry her back to the bed.

But he couldn't. Not now. He needed to take care of some unfinished business.

Lizzie immediately seemed to sense his withdrawal and released her embrace.

"I've got to go," he said quietly.

She nodded, glancing at the floor before blinking back up to look into his eyes. Exploring. Seeking. But nowhere did he see judgment.

He went to put on his boots and then picked up his jacket and shrugged into it.

"And the coffee?" Lizzie asked, not having moved from the kitchen area.

"I made that for you."

How LONG had it been since he'd visited the store? Ten months, he realized, just before he'd left town. He sat outside in his car, taking in the exterior of the place and watching a plow make quick work of the snow in the lot that served several businesses.

It seemed strange being there now. Although he'd been back in town for some time, he'd made a point of avoiding the area. Avoiding any thought connected with it.

For three years this place and his partners, Nina and Kevin, had been an everyday part of his life. Begun when they decided one day over lunch at Nina's café to combine their three separate businesses into one mammoth one. All it had entailed was signing a few papers and breaking down a few walls.

Gauge rubbed the back of his neck, realizing that the physical walls weren't the only ones that had come down. For the first time in a long time, he'd let down a few of his emotional barriers. Allowed Nina and Kevin past defenses that had taken a lifetime of disappointment to build up and fortify. And for a short time he'd gotten a taste of what a family, a real family, was like.

At least until the day he'd proposed a night of anonymous sex to Nina…and encouraged Kevin, who'd always secretly been in love with her, to be the man to meet her.

He shook his head to clear the memory and climbed out of the car, the biting December air penetrating his clothes.

Signs of Christmas were everywhere. White lights blinking. Red bows blowing in the wind. Bells both big and small ringing. As a kid, Christmas Day had loomed much like any other to him. Usually he and his father would hang around the motel room, waiting for the hours to pass, watching TV. Maybe they'd go out for a turkey dinner at a nearby diner in whatever town they happened to be in.

If he was lucky, his father would give him a gift. One year, it had been a leather coat. Another a pair of boots. Mostly practical items that wouldn't take up too much room in the car and didn't cost too much, because there wasn't much money to spend.

He'd never really bought anyone a gift until the first Christmas Eve that he and Nina and Kevin had spent together. He'd found a rare edition of a Mark Twain novel for Kevin, and had bought Nina a gold necklace with cooking utensil charms on it.

What they had given him in return had been more than anything anyone could have bought: They'd given him inclusion and unconditional love.

Until he'd broken their trust by taking advantage of a vulnerable and confused Nina, who'd seemed to think he was her anonymous lover, not Kevin.

He stopped in front of the store and stared at the closed sign. They didn't officially open until eleven on Sundays, but he knew Nina would be there. He looked at the windows above the store where she used to have her apartment. Now it was seeing her car parked in the lot that told him she was there, since she had moved into Kevin's house after they married. He tried the door to find it locked and then knocked.

Almost immediately he saw Nina emerge from the

entryway to the music center, probably coming from the café beyond, and he was swept into the past, when he'd watched her make the journey several times a day. She paused for a moment on the other side of the glass, holding his gaze, then looked behind her before stepping forward to unlock the doors.

"I got your message," he said simply.

"Sure. Yes." She closed the door and locked it again, visually sweeping the parking lot. "Why didn't you use your key?"

It honestly hadn't occurred to him. "You alone?"

"Um, yes. Kevin should be in soon. I had to come in to get the normal morning baking out of the way." She passed him. "Come on. I have some sticky buns in the oven."

He followed, watching her own personal set of nicely rounded buns, even though he told himself he shouldn't. Hey, he was only human. And a man at that. Surely looking never hurt anybody.

They started walking through the music center and he paused, taking in the many changes that had been made. Where he had favored darker, more intimate lighting, fluorescent bulbs had been installed, brightening the area. His posters of classic blues and rock icons had been exchanged for life-size stand-up cardboard cutouts of current pop sensations. He stopped in front of one of Britney Spears and frowned.

"The new manager had his own ideas."

He nodded. Hey, while he might still own a third of the shop, he'd forfeited his right to say how the place should be run when he'd left town ten months ago. It wasn't his space anymore.

"Making more money?"

Nina stood in the doorway to the café, watching him. "Profits of the music center are up fifteen percent."

He raised his eyebrows and then nodded. Nothing like being told that someone else was doing a better job than he had.

"Come on," she said, turning again.

Gauge followed, the hollow feeling in his stomach beginning to grow.

Nina disappeared into the kitchen and he opened the door, watching her take the buns out of the oven, big, red oven mitts on her hands. She donned a snowy-white apron over her standard uniform of black stretchy pants and white, short-sleeved shirt, everything hugging her slender body to sleek perfection. She took the mitts off and then slathered the sticky glaze on top of the fresh buns.

How many mornings and evenings had the three of them hung around in this kitchen in the café or the large, stone fireplace in the bookstore, just chatting and enjoying one another's company? It seemed to have been just yesterday, yet at the same time years ago.

"Want one?" Nina asked, breaking off one of the buns and putting it on a plate. She placed it on the stainless-steel prep island close to where he stood.

Gauge released the door so that it could close and stepped fully inside the kitchen. "Thanks."

She shot a brief smile at him, appearing to be going out of her way not to meet his gaze as she put in another batch of baking and took out a finished tray. She frowned, testing for doneness. "Damn oven. It's been acting up for a couple of days now."

"Would it be better if I came back later?" he asked.

"What?" His question had apparently caught her up short. Finally, she ceased her nonstop activity. She grasped the edge of the counter, took a deep breath and then smiled, meeting his gaze. "Sorry. Things have been hectic around here, what with the Christmas rush and losing Heidi to her catering company. I didn't expect you so soon, that's all. I guess maybe I was hoping you'd call so we could meet when…"

"When Kevin's around?"

She caught her bottom lip between her teeth then nodded. "Yeah."

She fidgeted with her left hand. Gauge realized she was moving her wedding ring back and forth.

"How about some coffee to go with that roll?" she asked.

She started past him to go back out into the café area. Gauge caught her arm.

He took in the catch of her breath, her hard swallow and the widening of her pupils as she stared at the door rather than at him.

He knew in that one moment that if he wanted to, he could pull her into his arms and she'd come.

The realization hit him with the force of a bulldozer.

Could she really still be attracted to him? Drawn to him the way he was to her? Why? She'd taken vows with another man. A man he knew she loved. Kevin. A best friend to both of them.

No matter how much he might have liked to test the possibility, he instead picked up her left hand and admired the wedding band there, along with a rock the size of Gibraltar. She deserved the largest diamond ever mined.

He released her hand. "It suits you."

She blinked at him curiously. "What?"

"The ring…being married. It suits you."

Her chin dipped as she smiled. "Thanks."

He reached out and held the door open for her, and could hear her sigh of relief as she passed him.

Moments later both of them sat safely at the counter, near enough to touch but purposely not touching.

Gauge felt he'd passed some sort of test. Not of Nina's making, but of his own. When he'd refused to act on the rush of testosterone in the kitchen, he'd broken through a threshold he hadn't known had been waiting for him.

"So," Nina said, smiling into her coffee mug. "I hear that Kevin came to see you the other day."

Gauge had hoped Kevin wouldn't have entered their conversation so early. The problem was, Kevin was the main issue between them.

Or was he?

No. Nina was trying to make it Kevin, but the truth was he and Nina had their own business to attend to. And until they did, no one was going to move forward.

"Yeah," Gauge said. "He came to see me. Came close to finally hitting me."

She looked alarmed.

"Don't worry. He kept his ever-present cool."

She didn't say anything for a long moment. Merely held on to her coffee cup until her knuckles whitened. "And you?"

Now there was a question. "I tried like hell to taunt him into knocking my lights out."

"Of course."

Gauge went silent, looking around at everything that was familiar, and those things that weren't.

Then he asked the question that he'd come there to ask. "That night…"

Nina went instantly stiff.

"Don't you think it's time that we both stopped pretending? You knew as much as I did that Kevin was the mystery man. So why did you sleep with me?"

12

GAUGE WASN'T one for scrounging around in the past for an answer he needed today. He'd come to learn that the past was best left where it was.

At least that's what he used to believe.

Now…

Well, now, he wanted…no, needed, to continue rebuilding that bridge he'd started three years ago.

Nina didn't respond to his question. At least not verbally. Physically, her every movement gave away her uneasiness.

"I don't know that I'm following you," she finally said, looking everywhere but at him.

Gauge felt defeat settle in around him. If he couldn't convince her to confront what had really happened between the three of them ten months ago, he held out little hope of repairing their relationship.

"Come on, Nina," he said quietly. "You can't tell me that in your heart of hearts, you didn't know that Kevin was the man you'd slept with. And that when you came to me—"

She quickly held up her hand. "No. Please. Stop."

He turned toward her. "No. I can't. Whatever's said here stays here. Between us. Between you and me. But we need to talk about this. You need to understand the role you played in what happened that night."

"A mistake happened."

Gauge winced, feeling as if she'd just sucker punched him.

And she had. Not physically, of course. But she'd landed an emotional wallop that was even more effective.

And the frustrating and saddening thing of it was, she knew it.

He started to get up. "Then I guess we have nothing to talk about. Don't call me. I won't call you."

"Gauge, wait." She reached out, grasping his coat sleeve. It was a light touch, but could have been a handcuff for all the control Gauge had over his own response.

He stopped, waiting.

"I don't know. Obviously you've been thinking a lot about that night."

"And you haven't?"

She looked down and nodded.

"And what conclusion have you come to, Nina? Beyond recognizing it as the mistake we all know it was."

She blinked up at him. "I…I…" She took a deep breath and let it out slowly, then laughed without humor. "You're really not going to back down from this, are you?"

He shook his head.

She appeared a blink away from tears.

Gauge reached out and cupped her face in his hand.

"Look, Nina. I'm not trying to hurt you. I came back to Fantasy to try to fix things. Make my way back to where we were."

She narrowed her gaze.

"Not that night. No, before then. Before you and I slept together."

She appeared relieved but only marginally.

"And if we stand a chance of doing that—and I think even you're coming to realize it's a long shot—then we have to understand why we did what we did."

She grasped her coffee mug again. "You're right."

Gauge sat back down and pretended an interest in his own coffee.

"So…where do we start?"

"Probably at the beginning."

SOMETIME LATER, Gauge felt better than he had in a long time. And he recognized that it wasn't only understanding that needed to happen, but acceptance. He felt that he and Nina had made great strides toward that end.

The problem was they'd forgotten about one other person: Kevin.

They heard the footsteps before either of them had a chance to react. Gauge had just said something in response to Nina and she had leaned into him much as she once had, laughing.

Nina looked over her shoulder at her husband and Gauge followed her gaze. Kevin's face was drawn tight as he gave them a once-over and then turned to walk back toward the bookstore without saying anything.

Thankfully, Nina didn't get up to run after him. She didn't even seem that concerned about his being upset.

Gauge would like to think it was because of the inroads they'd made that morning.

Nina's soft sigh spoke of her frustration when it came to her husband. "Do you think you two will ever be able to work this out?"

Gauge tilted his cup to find it empty. "I don't know, Nina. I don't know."

She touched his upper arm and squeezed. "Yes, well, I want you to make it right. I miss you. I miss us as a threesome."

He grinned at her.

Rather than blushing or acting coy, she smacked his arm and laughed in a teasing manner that told him that the two of them had definitely turned a corner for good.

"Get your mind out of the gutter, Patrick Gauge."

"Never."

LIZZIE SPENT the better part of the morning back at her house feeling…odd. As if something important was left hanging in the air, just out of her reach. But it was going to take Gauge's cooperation in order to reach it.

She glanced away from the Christmas cards she was hand addressing toward the garage and the apartment above it for the fifth time in so many minutes.

"Oh, just stop it," she ordered herself, putting double the energy into her card-writing efforts.

Her brother, Jesse, had called, asking if she had some coffee to spare. She'd readily invited him over. Anything to keep from wondering where Gauge had gone. And if he was going to help her reach that something important. Or leave it hanging there forever.

Of course, it only stood to reason that Jesse would arrive and Gauge would return at the same time.

She watched as her brother drove his pickup down the driveway, stopping just short of the garage so he could come in the back, as all of them had been taught to do at their parents'. Just as he was getting out, Gauge was walking to his place. The two men shook hands, and Gauge glanced toward the window and gave a wave before disappearing up the stairs.

Damn.

Damn, damn, damn.

Jesse and his bad timing. Would things ever change?

She opened the back door before he reached it and directed him to wipe his boots on the rug there. She looked to see if Gauge was still in view. He wasn't. She closed the door.

"He's still here, huh?" Jesse asked.

Since it had been Jesse's ex-girlfriend Heidi who had recommended Gauge for the place, her brother was familiar with him. That, and the fact Jesse seemed to have spent the better part of his adult years in the pub where Gauge occasionally played, though she understood he still partially owned the BMC.

Lizzie stretched up on tiptoe to kiss her younger brother. "How's it going, kiddo?"

Even though only a few years separated them, it seemed like more to her. Her mother had told her it had something to do with emotional intelligence. That men didn't age as quickly as their female counterparts. But Lizzie was beginning to wonder if it was just the way they were made.

"Hey, yourself." He gave her a once-over as he shrugged out of his sheepskin coat and hung it on a hook near the door. "You look good. Did you go to church or something?"

"Mmm. Or something."

She wasn't dressed especially nice. Liar. Okay, so she had put on a nice pair of slacks and a black cashmere sweater that kept slipping down over either one or the other of her shoulders.

"Coffee?"

"I'd prefer a beer if you got one."

"I thought you came for coffee." She looked to find it after noon and took a beer from the fridge. She kept his favorite brand especially for him.

"I was talking figuratively."

"Right. Well, you don't mind if I have coffee since I made it already."

"Not at all."

He walked into the family room as she fixed herself a fresh cup of coffee and then switched off the maker. She'd already had two cups and should probably pass on another, but seeing as she hadn't gotten a whole hell of a lot of sleep the night before, she figured it couldn't hurt.

She took a seat on the couch next to Jesse, who was going through her cards.

"Why are you sending one to the Wilsons? Doesn't Mom say they're the rudest couple on earth?"

"Yes, but she also sends them a card every year, too."

He gave her a "whatever" nod and then settled back on his side of the couch. "So I hear you and the parents had an interesting run-in the other day."

"Annie has a big mouth."

"And that's news how?"

Lizzie laughed. "Got me there. I just hope she waited until the kids were out of the room before she said something."

"Right. No point damaging their lives like our parents did ours."

Lizzie took a sip of her coffee and then put it down on the table. "So what brings you around my way? Has something happened with Mom and Dad?"

"You mean, beyond their continued World War Three battle plans?" He shook his head. "No. Nothing on that front."

Lizzie grimaced. She should have stopped hoping something would have happened by now. That some sort of lightbulb would go off above their heads and make them realize they were still in love and should remain a couple.

This from the most unromantic woman in existence, if you listened to her friend Tabby.

"No, I came to ask your advice on something."

Lizzie curled her right leg under her and faced him better. "Shoot."

"It's about Mona."

She pretended neutrality at the mention of her brother's new girlfriend but must have missed the mark.

Jesse tsked. "What is it with you guys and Mona? Why don't you like her?"

"I never said I don't like her." She'd just liked Heidi, his ex-fiancé, better.

"You don't have to. It's written all over your face whenever I bring up her name."

Lizzie sighed. "I'm sorry, Jesse. I guess maybe we just need a little time. You know, to get to know her."

"She's been around far more often than Heidi ever was."

"Maybe that's the problem."

Jesse squinted at her, looking so much like the handsome kid she remembered growing up. "How so?"

"I'm just saying that I'm surprised you didn't bring her along with you here today, that's all. Everywhere you go, she goes."

"She's my girlfriend."

"So she is.

"So why isn't she here today?"

Jesse looked down at his clasped hands. "She's mad at me because I forgot our three-year anniversary."

"Three-year anniversary? You guys have only been a couple for the past few months."

"Yeah, I know. She's counting from the time we met in Boston."

Lizzie forced herself not to say anything. Mona was including, of course, the time Jesse had officially been engaged to Heidi.

"Anyway, that's not why I'm here. I don't give a flying fig if any of you like her. I love her. And you're just going to have to deal with it."

Lizzie nodded, praying that Mona finally delivered on her frequent threats to head back to Boston…alone.

"I want you to help me come up with a really unique way to propose to her on Christmas Eve…."

Lizzie looked around for something to hit him with but came up short. "Don't you think it's a little too soon?"

He glared at her.

"Oh, right," she said. "It's been three years." She drummed her fingers against the sofa back and tried to pretend that she was concentrating. "I'd have to say that if you want to be unique, you shouldn't propose on Christmas Eve then."

"God, I should have known you'd say something like that. You're all just hell-bent on trying to get us to break up, aren't you?"

Lizzie leaned forward, affronted. "Jesse, it wasn't that long ago that you were engaged to be married to someone else."

"Someone else who's now marrying my best friend."

"Oh. Yes. Right." She waved her hand. "Anyway, that's not what we're talking about." She sat back and sighed. "Look, you just said you wanted it to be unique, didn't you?"

"Really unique."

"Right. Really unique." She turned her hands palms up. "Then that means not proposing on any of the days that other holidays are celebrated. You know, like Valentine's Day, birthdays, Halloween, Christmas…" She counted them off on her fingers.

Jesse blinked at her. "Mona told me that if she doesn't get an engagement ring on Christmas, she's going back to Boston."

The words *let her,* followed by a loud hooray, weren't going to get her anywhere, so she bit her tongue.

"So what's keeping you from doing it today?"

He appeared spellbound. "What?"

She shrugged and reached for her coffee cup, unable to believe she was helping her brother propose to a woman who had to be the biggest slut, the most manipulative shrew Lizzie had ever met. No matter how sexy she was. "Sure. It's your third anniversary, right? So propose to her today. Now. Go out and buy her a great ring—"

"The biggest."

She gave an eye roll. "Right. The biggest ring you can afford," she said, putting emphasis on the last word. "Go back and tell her to get ready, and then take her out somewhere so you can propose."

"Where?"

"I don't know! God, do you want me to cinch the deal by sleeping with her, too?"

Jesse flashed a grin. The same grin that had nearly every woman he met swooning for the chance to go out with him. And here he'd brought a slut back from Boston.

"I've got it!" he said.

"Great," Lizzie muttered.

"I'll take her sledding."

"Sledding as in 'trudging up a hill and getting all covered with snow' sledding?"

"Yeah. She won't expect anything then."

"And she'll probably shove your face in the snow." Lizzie tapped her finger against her lips. "Take her sleigh riding."

It seemed to take him a moment to lock on to what she was saying.

"Yes," she said, leaning forward and warming to her own idea. "Go to Mom and Dad's and get the thickest, softest, nicest blanket you can find, pick up a bottle of champagne and a couple of glasses, and tell her it's to celebrate your anniversary…only the gift you'll give her is a proposal."

Jesse catapulted from the couch. "Perfect!"

He pulled her up from the couch and gave her a big hug, swinging her around in a circle. "Thanks, sis." He kissed her loudly on the cheek. "I knew you'd come through for me."

"Yes, well…whatever."

He chuckled as he grabbed his coat in the kitchen and opened the door.

"Good luck!" she called after him.

She wasn't sure if he heard, since he practically ran for his car, nearly slipping on the ice as he went.

Lizzie pulled her sweater up where it had slid down her shoulder again, watching as Jesse backed out. Then she switched her gaze to the apartment over the garage, wondering if she should trek out and see Gauge.

Instead she slowly closed the door and decided she'd wait and let him come to see her.

13

MUCH LATER that afternoon, Lizzie lay back in her bed watching dusk begin to darken the eastern sky, the top sheet sliding from her naked right breast…a breast that Gauge instantly took into his mouth and suckled, reigniting the fire that seemed to forever be in her belly whenever he was nearby.

Oh, Gauge had come over to the house, all right. A scant five minutes after Jesse had left. And the two of them had been in bed in the hours since.

"Mmm." Lizzie arched her back, stretching her sore muscles and reaching for a piece of blue cheese from a tray she'd prepared during a break earlier and put on the side table. "You can't possibly be ready to go again."

Gauge leisurely licked her nipple, then pulled the sheet from her left breast and gave that nipple equal time. Lizzie wriggled as the pressure built between her legs.

Gauge plopped back down onto the pillow next to hers and they both lay staring at the ceiling. "You're right. It's going to take another minute or two."

Lizzie laughed and tossed a grape his way. It landed

on his stomach, where he trapped it with his hand. Picking it up, he sucked on it briefly, and then tunneled his hand under the sheet. Lizzie gasped when she felt the cold fruit make contact with her overheated genitals. Then she spread her thighs to give him better access.

He rolled the grape around her clit and then down and back up again.

Then he took his hand out and ate the grape.

"You naughty, naughty boy, you," she murmured, now ready for another round herself as she rolled to her side and kissed him.

He returned her kiss while chewing on the grape until she ended up with a portion of it in her mouth.

Then she collapsed next to him and groaned. "I don't think there's a single part of me that doesn't hurt or pulse or both."

"That's a good thing."

Lizzie smiled from ear to ear. "That's definitely a good thing."

"So, I didn't get a chance to ask you earlier. What did your brother want?"

"Mmm. He was soliciting advice on how to propose to his whore of a girlfriend."

Gauge's laugh was so unexpected it made Lizzie grin, though she kept her eyes closed and nestled her head deeper into her pillow.

"Mona's not a whore," he said. "She's a woman who knows her sexual power and isn't afraid to use it."

"That's right. I forgot that you already know her. You know, her being the bar slut that she is."

He chuckled again. "And here I thought you were the nonjudgmental type."

"Me? The successful trial attorney?"

"Mmm. Stupid of me."

"Blame my parents. Only a couple named Bonnie and Clyde would have a Lizzie, Annie and Jesse as children. Seems I've been trying to buck expectations since the day I was born."

She opened her eyes and stared at the ceiling and the three pools of light for long moments. Gauge had decided he'd had enough of the dark last night and had turned on the lamps, wanting to watch her face when she came.

"Gauge?"

"Hmm?"

"Are you sleeping?"

"Not yet."

She heard the sheets rustle.

"What is it?"

"Nothing. It's just that, do you ever wonder if love is just something we convince ourselves to feel?"

She realized she'd just introduced the ultimate four-letter word into a bed that had been reserved solely for sex.

"Not us," she said quickly. "I'm thinking about my brother…my parents…."

She forced herself to look over at him, to make sure he hadn't taken her words wrong. She found him staring contemplatively at the ceiling, his hand against hers, absently rubbing it.

"I don't know," he said. "It could be."

His response made her feel better. She relaxed again and entwined her fingers with his. "I mean, just look at my parents. They're supposed to be in the middle of a divorce…scratch that, they *are* in the middle of a divorce after thirty years of marriage, and yet every time my sister or brother or I turn around, they're having sex somewhere or other in the house."

She moved her head toward Gauge at the same time he looked at her.

She burst out laughing. "I know. TMI. Welcome to my life. I can't remember a time when one of us didn't stumble upon them. The other day I caught them in my old bedroom with leather and feather."

He rolled to his side and propped his head up on his hand. "Sounds like an idea to me."

Lizzie made a face. "I don't think I could get the picture of the two of them out of my head long enough to enjoy myself."

Gauge trailed his fingertips over her shoulder blades, into the valley between her breasts, around her nipples, and then down to circle her navel. She shivered. "Oh, I don't know," he said quietly, leaning over to blow in her ear. "I think I could make you forget."

She smiled at him. "You know what I mean."

"Yes. I think I do. The same thing used to happen with me when it came to my father."

His expression seemed faraway.

"Oh?"

"Mmm. Since we were on the road so much, and my dad didn't make much money as bass player in whatever band he'd temporarily hooked up with, we always shared a motel room." He focused on her and grinned. "You can't imagine how many times I walked in on him. Or woke up in the middle of the night to sounds of sex from the next bed. Or went into the bathroom to find a strange woman in the shower or on the commode."

"You're kidding?"

"Nope. Lost my virginity to one of those women when I was thirteen. She had some fantasy of being a virgin's first. And I...well, I was thirteen."

Yikes.

Lizzie was transfixed, listening to him tell the story as if he were a visitor from another planet and was casually talking about the weather.

"And here I've been used to being the odd one out with horny parents. Never mind that they're named Bonnie and Clyde and named their kids after notorious outlaws."

"Did they ever have sex somewhere where they knew you'd find them?"

"What, like exhibitionists? No. They just liked to have sex, I guess. And when you have three kids running around the place, you're bound to get caught."

Gauge reached for another grape. She gasped when he pressed it against her right nipple.

"But enough about me. You apparently have me beat hands down on childhood horror stories."

He rolled the grape over to her other nipple, following the cold trail with the warmth of his tongue. Not with any destination in particular, merely appearing to enjoy the journey. "I don't see them as horror stories. My life was what it was. And I knew I was lucky to have it."

"Lucky?" She watched him move the grape down to her navel, where he left it and reached for another one.

"Mmm."

"If you guys traveled so much, did you go to school?"

"When I could."

Lizzie raised her brows. She had almost nineteen years of school, all told, what with getting her bachelor's and then her law degree. "Did you graduate?"

"I passed the GED." He grinned at her. "I also have a few semesters of college. Music mostly. Some literature. Not enough credits in either for a degree, but not too far off."

She couldn't remember seeing any books in his apartment. He told her one of the first places he checked out in a new town was the local library.

"Where's your father now?"

He fell silent.

And Lizzie wished she could take the words back…

WHERE WAS HIS FATHER NOW, indeed…

Everyone had parents. It was a fact of life that it took a man's sperm to fertilize a woman's egg. Yes, he had parents. Biologically speaking. And he supposed his father had done the best he could. Most times Gauge was satisfied with leaving it at that.

Then there were times when he wondered what if.

What if his parents had been a couple rather than a one-night stand that had resulted in a pregnancy and pretty much an unwanted child? What if his mother hadn't dumped him on his father's doorstep when he was six? What if he'd had a normal upbringing in a normal neighborhood and gone to a normal school, rather than living the vagabond lifestyle he'd come to know, if not love?

"There's a lot to be said for the way I was raised," he found himself saying quietly. "I've traveled to a lot of places. Learned firsthand what might take others years to understand about music. Met some incredible people. Jimmy Witherspoon, Bo Diddley, John Lee Hooker, Stevie Ray Vaughan…I mean, man. What talent. I'd listen to any one of these guys and spend the next month trying to emulate them on my secondhand acoustic guitar…."

He paused, snapshots from different bars, different blues players, smiles and laughter coalescing into a musical collage.

"When I was a teen, I didn't have a curfew or rules. I could do pretty much what I wanted when I wanted. Every teenager's dream, I'm told."

At the time, he hadn't known any better. Sure, through television shows he watched, and some of the other kids he came in contact with, he understood that the way he and his father lived wasn't the way everyone lived. But it had been his reality. It was completely normal for him to sit at a beat-up table in the back of a bar during the day going over his math homework with a waitress while his father practiced with the band.

Meals were grabbed when he or his father thought about it, often bar fare serving to tide him over. He'd once gone five days with nothing more than peanuts and pretzels as nutrition, and orange juice that was meant to be mixed with alcohol.

When he was too young to play in the band, he'd swept floors and cleaned out toilets and was once awakened at one in the morning in a motel to go clean up vomit in the men's room of the bar because the waitress refused to do it.

He'd been nine and hadn't thought anything unusual about the request. He'd merely done the job and pocketed the two bucks the owner gave him.

"My father was a good man," he said aloud. "'I ain't never hit a woman, or hurt a child,' he used to say. Of course, later on, he'd added the word *intentionally* to the latter part of the statement because he'd fathered at least three other children with three other women that he knew about. All of them in different parts of the country."

He glanced at Lizzie to find her shocked or fascinated or a combination of both.

"Do you… I mean, have you fathered any children?" she whispered.

"Me?" He smiled. "No. As soon as my father figured out I was sexually active, he threw a box of condoms at me. Told me not to make the same mistakes he did."

Lizzie cringed. "Ouch."

"Tell me about it." He rubbed a small, narrow scar

just above his right eyebrow. "This is where the corner of the box hit me."

He fell silent for a minute, marveling at all he'd told her. At how easy it was to let the memories flow out like water from a rusty can.

She curled closer to his side and he slid his arm under her head and rubbed her arm. So soft.

"So you haven't said where he is now. Your father, I mean."

Gauge's throat tightened. "He's in Saint Louis."

"Is he still playing?"

He gave a lopsided smile as he imagined his old man playing bass guitar in heaven. "Maybe." He turned his head to look down at her. "He's buried in a small church graveyard just outside East Saint Louis."

"Oh, God. I'm sorry. I didn't know… I mean, I assumed…"

"Don't be sorry. You didn't kill him. Booze did."

He'd had no idea his father was ill. There was nothing to suggest there was anything wrong with him. If he moved a little slow, Gauge had guessed it was because he was getting older. If he clutched his side every now and again, he'd say it must have been something he ate. Or maybe it was those damn kidney stones his own father used to have.

Then came the day Gauge had come back from trying to charm one of the town girls outside a private school a couple of miles away. He needed to get his father up so he could go pick up his pay from the bar…but his dad wouldn't wake up.

He'd been sixteen. No other family that he knew of outside the kid in Arizona. And no idea where he went from there.

"His old beat-up truck and his guitar and a half-empty bottle of Jack is about all he left me."

He heard Lizzie's thick swallow and looked down to find her eyes bright with tears.

"Shh," he said, wiping her cheek with his thumb. "That was a long time ago. And I'm here now. And okay."

"I know," she said haltingly, as if doubting her ability to speak. "It's just… God, that must have been so hard for you."

"It wasn't easy. But like I said, it was what it was." He continued stroking the soft skin of her back. "I stepped in to play for my father that night. Everyone chipped in to help bury him. And two days later, I stood over his grave with the waitress that had been his stop-over lover."

"What did you do after that?"

"What we did together before. I went from town to town, gig to gig. Turning down any offers of a permanent spot in a band in exchange for a change of scenery and a different bed and different woman every other week or so."

Lizzie curved her arm around him and squeezed, kissing his neck. "Was there never anyone special?"

"Once." He squinted at the ceiling. "Maybe twice." If you counted Nina, he silently added. And he did.

Then there was the woman in his arms. It was still too soon to say whether anything would come of his and

Lizzie's affair. But the mere fact that he'd shared what he had, that she'd found a way to coax it out of him, spoke volumes.

And when it came to sex, she definitely ranked right up there with the best. Inventive. Wanton. And thoroughly insatiable.

"How did you end up here in Fantasy?"

He chuckled softly and kissed her. "Let's just say that there was something tempting about fulfilling all my fantasies in Fantasy."

She smiled as she shifted her left leg over his and then slid on top of him, straddling him even as she kissed him.

"Let's see what I can do to help…."

LIZZIE GASPED when Gauge turned her back over, wedging his hips between her thighs. She felt his hard, thick erection pulsing against the tender folds of her womanhood, unprotected and hot.

She stared up into his face. Taking in the scar above his brow. Noting the other scars that he hadn't shared the origins of. Compassion for this man crashed over her, flowed through her, until all she knew was this one moment in time. This one instant when nothing else mattered.

She'd never known anyone with a past so different from hers. And that he had shared as much as he had touched a part of her deep inside. She combed his thick hair back from his forehead with her fingers, hotter for him than she could remember ever being for another man. And connected in a way she didn't want to explore.

He reached for the bedside table and plucked a grape from the plate. He placed it between her lips. She bit into the fleshy fruit and then welcomed his kiss. He pulled away and she swallowed, watching as he took another grape and placed it on her breastbone. She fought to regulate her breathing, transfixed as he used his nose to nudge the fruit down between her breasts, licking her skin as he went.

THE RINGING OF THE FRONT DOORBELL roused Lizzie from a state that teetered between wakefulness and sleep. Gauge's arm was around her waist, pulling her backside to his front.

"Expecting company?" he murmured.

She glanced at the clock. Just after seven. Gauge would have to be leaving soon.

She ignored the doorbell and snuggled closer to him, wiggling her bottom against his semiaroused member. "I don't want to get up."

"So don't."

The shrill ring of the doorbell sounded again, as if in response to his comment.

Lizzie groaned. "Whoever it is knows I'm home. Probably they saw the lights on up here. And my car's in the garage."

"So?"

She closed her eyes and smiled. Was life really so simple?

Yes, she realized. It could be if she wanted it to.

Then the different options of who the visitor might be ran through her mind. She'd set the home phone to privacy so all calls went directly to voice mail. And her cell phone was down in the family room on vibrate. The only sure way anyone could get in contact with her in case of emergency was if they came to her house.

She thought of her brother, who might have taken his girlfriend on that sleigh ride to propose. Could the horse have bolted and Mona broken her neck? One could only hope. Then again, it could have been Jesse who'd been hurt.

Then there was the whole situation with her parents.

She groaned again and wriggled out of Gauge's arms, grabbing her robe from the post at the foot of the bed where she'd left it earlier to get the cheese plate. He rolled to his back and folded his arms behind his head, looking like a Greek god as he watched her. A scraggly, battle-scarred Greek god with tattoos and, she was learning, a heart of gold.

"Sorry. I've got to get this."

"By all means," he said with a grin. "Mind if I use your shower?"

"Go ahead."

She put her slippers on and tied her belt as she went. The humongous one-size-fits-all Turkish terry-cloth robe was the one she'd bought from a hotel in Chicago and big enough to cover everything.

Well, everything but the stubble burn she felt on her chin and neck. But that was okay. She could always claim she wasn't feeling well. That would justify a day in bed as easily as the reality.

Although the reality was much better than any fantasy she could have concocted.

She hurried down the stairs and pulled open the door in the middle of the next ring.

And stood staring at the last person she'd expected to find there.

"Jerry!"

14

LIZZIE COULDN'T HAVE BEEN more surprised had the pope been standing on her doorstep. It took a full minute for the reality of the situation to sink in. Her ex-boyfriend, who'd dumped her via text message two weeks ago, was there...and her new boyfriend was upstairs in her bedroom.

The facts were dizzying.

She expected him to look at her and know instantly what she'd been up to. Instead, Jerry brushed right by her into the house, something in a brown paper bag tucked under his arm.

"What took you so long? It's freezing out there."

He turned to face her and Lizzie closed the door after him, trying to decide what her options were. But she was slow to come up with any answers.

Jerry grinned and held out his right hand. "I'm free, baby. I've left her for good this time."

Lizzie made herself blink.

Had he just said what she thought he had?

He put the bag down on the foyer table. "I just couldn't be there anymore. Not after I realized that this is where I want to be. That you're the one I love. Not her."

Lizzie stared at him, as if incapable of bringing him or his words into focus. Worse, she completely failed to relate what he was saying to her current predicament.

And he couldn't have been more oblivious to her condition had he worn a blindfold.

She watched as he took out the item from the bag. Her waffle maker.

"Jerry," she said quietly.

He appeared not to hear her as he looked around. "I never realized how much this place feels like home."

"Jerry," she repeated, more loudly.

"These past two weeks have been hell." He started shrugging out of his London Fog overcoat. A coat she'd helped him pick out. "I've missed you."

"Jerry!" she almost shouted.

He blinked at her as if she'd punched him in the stomach.

Lizzie could now see the man she'd spent so much of her life convincing herself that she loved in a new light. He was handsome enough with his light brown hair and pale green eyes. Working out at the gym guaranteed he had a nice body. An expensive dentist had given him an expensive smile.

But somehow she'd never recognized the…useless air that clung to him like his expensive cologne. A clueless bearing that made him seem to work on autopilot. He hadn't looked directly at her once since she'd opened the door. Probably because he was concerned about what she might say if given half the chance.

Then again, no. That would be giving him too much credit. Instead, his shallowness rendered him immune to any and everyone around him as he went about his own business, expecting the world to expand and contract to accommodate him.

"What are you doing here?" she asked, now that she finally had his attention.

He glanced over at her then looked at his watch. "What are you doing in a robe at seven o'clock on a Sunday night?"

No, *Are you feeling all right? Is everything okay?* Instead, he'd chosen to couch his remark in a way that might have made her feel underdressed two weeks ago.

Now it made her mad.

"Answer my question, Jerry."

"What question?" He folded his coat over his arm. Probably because he'd have to get by her in order to hang it up in the closet.

"What are you doing here?"

"I told you, baby." He stepped toward her, putting on his best grin. "I've come back to you."

Movement in the upstairs hall caught Lizzie's attention. She gasped at the sight of Gauge, still completely nude at the stop of the stairs, leaning against the wall, his arms crossed.

Before she could recover enough to distract Jerry, her usually clueless ex turned to follow her gaze.

Gauge crossed his feet at the ankles, his semierect

penis curving down his right thigh for God and everyone to see.

Lizzie wished the robe would swallow her whole.

Jerry narrowed his eyes, as if unable to believe what he was seeing. Much the way Lizzie had looked at him as he'd brushed his way inside her house.

Gauge gave a little wave.

Lizzie was instantly furious with two men rather than one.

A LITTLE WHILE LATER, Lizzie paced back and forth in her bedroom, trying to get a handle on her emotions. Jerry had left—shocker—taking his waffle maker with him. Gauge had gone on to take his shower—double shocker—and she was left to sort through things on her own as she listened to Jerry's BMW peel rubber out of her shoveled driveway and the sound of the shower in the master bedroom where Gauge stood under the spray naked.

Had the world gone insane? It was difficult to believe that her life could take a complete one-eighty in such a short period of time. One minute she'd been connecting to Gauge in a way she hadn't known it was possible to with another human being…the next she was looking for the exit to a ride that she would never have boarded had she known how dangerous the dips and turns were.

Finally, she plopped down on her bed. She stared at the twisted sheets under her feet and pulled at them almost violently. She nearly spilled onto the floor as she tugged until she could throw them back over the bed she'd spent the afternoon with Gauge in.

She knew a moment of pause as she rested her hand against the mattress.

Gauge headed back into the bedroom, rubbing a towel against his hair, completely dressed. She snapped her hand back from the bed as if burned.

She stared at him and he stopped his approach and leaned against the bathroom doorjamb.

"What were you thinking?" she asked in a half whisper.

He didn't say anything for a long moment. Then he tossed the towel to the counter behind him and walked over to sit in an armchair near the cold fireplace. He moved his boots toward him.

"Are you going to answer me?" she repeated, wondering if perhaps she only thought she was speaking aloud. Perhaps the one-sided conversation was taking place solely in her head.

"I wasn't thinking anything," he said, pulling one of his boots on and adjusting the bottom of his jeans over it. "I heard voices. It sounded like you were stressed. And I went to see what the trouble was."

"Then stood leaning against the wall wearing nothing but your dirty grin, looking like a feral wolf staking its territory."

His movements slowed as he put the other boot on. He finished and then planted his feet evenly on the floor. He looked directly at her. "I don't hide from anyone."

"Who asked you to hide? I'm not asking you to hide. But discretion would have been the better part of valor here."

"Sounds like hiding to me."

He rested his forearms on his knees and continued looking at her as she sat on the bed.

"You're angry."

Lizzie moved her mouth a couple of times but nothing came out. Then she sighed and ran her hand through her tousled hair. "I'm upset, yes."

"Upset that I'm here? Or upset that he left?"

"Neither. Both." She pushed off the bed and started pacing again, her bare feet moving from thick flokati rug to polished wood and back again. "I don't know."

Gauge watched her quietly. Then he got up, grabbed his jacket and stood looking at her. "Don't worry, Lizzie. He'll be back. Men always want what they can't have."

He turned to leave.

Lizzie was on him so quickly she surprised herself with her actions. She grasped his arm to stop him and then rounded to face him. "What?" The word was barely a whisper.

"Trust me. He'll be back."

"I don't want him back. That's not the point here."

He raised a brow in mocking question.

"The point is…" She dug in her heels, refusing to give in to the restless energy that packed her veins. "The point is, you took a decision away from me that was mine to make."

He remained silent. Doubtful.

"Don't you get it? It wasn't your job to chase Jerry away. It was mine to tell him why he couldn't stay. Why I didn't want him to stay."

"And if I hadn't been here?"

She mulled over that one.

"If you and I had never slept together? What would have happened then, Lizzie?"

As a trial attorney, she was used to giving good cross-examination. But not when it came to close personal relationships. That might even be the reason she'd chosen the branch of law she had, since her personal life was rife with things unsaid.

But apparently not now. No. Gauge wanted to engage her in a conversation she wasn't so sure she wanted to have just then.

He leaned in and kissed her. Slowly. Leisurely. Curving the fingers of his free hand along her jaw and staring deeply into her eyes.

"We both agreed from the beginning that this was just about sex, Lizzie. There's no changing the rules now."

She felt as if he'd taken one of the jagged icicles hanging from her eaves and stabbed it straight through her heart, even though there was a ring of truth in his words. It had been about sex. Hadn't both of them made that completely clear in the beginning?

But that had been then. This was now. Somewhere down the line, it had evolved into much, much more. Through the sex they'd knocked down barriers they hadn't known they'd erected and made inroads into virgin territory, surrendering parts of themselves no one had laid ownership to before. They were tied together.

Her lungs refused air. No. She was the one who had surrendered parts of herself to Gauge.

Apparently it had been entirely one-sided.

He stepped toward the door as she wrapped her arms around herself, watching him go.

He never looked back once.

15

DON'T WORRY. He'll be back. Men always want what they can't have.

The words, his words, resonated through Gauge's brain as he navigated his way through the next couple of days. Sunday night, he'd played with the band. Monday and tonight, he'd made sure to be out of his apartment by six, before Lizzie returned home from work, commandeering the stool at the end of the bar where others left him alone for the most part.

And he'd been right about men wanting what they couldn't have. Judging by his own tortured hell when it came to Nina…well, he couldn't compare what he felt now for Lizzie to Nina. Rather, he'd come to accept that what had gone down was basic human survival instincts at their worst.

For three years, he and Nina and Kevin had been friends. While they enjoyed flirting, it had been harmless and purposely platonic.

Then the dynamic had changed when Gauge had arranged for the one night of anonymous sex between Nina and Kevin.

In that one instant, Nina graduated from friend to a woman in play. She had been something for which to compete. Someone to woo and seduce. And Kevin had become his nemesis.

Gauge had long since learned that hormones could get men into all kinds of trouble. That the fundamental urge to spread their seed meant that they often intruded in others' territory, putting their very life at risk in the quest for a woman's affection.

Except he hadn't expected to have to vie for Lizzie's attention.

"One last one?" Charlie asked, holding a bottle of Jack up.

Gauge pushed his shot glass toward him. "Sure. Hit me."

He'd lost count of how many he'd downed. Not enough to quiet the voices in his head. Enough to blur the edges of the man opposite him.

"Why don't I drop you off on my way home?"

Gauge shook his head. He'd driven in far worse condition than this. And it was late. There would barely be a soul on the road for him to threaten.

"I'll take him."

Gauge glanced at the waitress who had slid up to sit on the stool next to him. She'd taken off her apron, revealing that the deep vee that had been visible even with it on was made by unbuttoning a cotton top, complementing the generous curve of her breasts. She was a brunette and pretty and nice.

And just what the bartender ordered.

LIZZIE SAT in front of the fireplace watching the last embers burn out, the chenille throw doing little to warm her from the cooling room. She couldn't sleep. Had gotten precious little of that essential commodity since Sunday and Jerry's unannounced visit and Gauge's territorial display.

She scratched her head and looked through the window at the garage again. It was dark. Just as it had been for the past two nights. She suspected that Gauge was avoiding her. Which was just as well, because she hadn't much wanted to see him.

Until now.

"Talk to him." Tabby's words from earlier in the evening haunted her.

"I can't. I don't know how. I mean, what do I say?"

"Tell him that you acted like an ass and that you're sorry."

This advice from a friend who had reminded her earlier on that this thing with Gauge was only a temporary fling. Pointing out that nothing serious could come from a relationship with a musician.

"But he's part owner of the store downtown," Lizzie had said.

"Oh, well, that changes everything. Propose marriage then."

She'd known her friend was being facetious. She also understood that if Tabby had her way, Lizzie would dump Gauge and move on, take the experience with him as it was, a run of great, short-term sex.

But Tabby didn't know what Lizzie did. Hadn't felt the connection that she had. Couldn't possibly understand.

"Maybe not. But what I do understand is that you have a bad habit of clinging to every man you date, no matter how bad he is for you."

Lizzie had winced at that one, and winced again at the memory.

"Jerry was always a jerk," Tabitha had gone on. "From day one. Yet you kept on seeing him, convinced yourself that he was The One. I was actually happy when he ran off and married that other idiot. But then last summer you started talking about how he'd left the idiot and was back in your life. And I couldn't help thinking, *Oh, no, here we go again.*"

"How come you didn't say anything?"

"Because you never asked me."

"And now?"

Tabitha had fallen silent, as if unprepared to give her opinion of the moment.

"You know, there's a saying that applies to people like you," Lizzie had told her. "Hindsight is always twenty-twenty."

"Maybe." To her surprise, her friend had sounded contrite. "I don't know. Let me ask you this. What would you have done had you not been seeing Gauge? Had he not come out, grabbed his Johnson and pissed all over Jerry's thousand-dollar shoes? Would you have taken Jerry back?"

Lizzie honestly couldn't say one way or another what she might have done. She only knew that she wouldn't take Jerry back now if he held a divorce decree in one hand and the biggest diamond on earth in the other.

But it seemed that Gauge had been right about Jerry coming back. Later that night, Jerry had called her.

She hadn't picked up, of course. He hadn't left a message on her home phone, but she had another text message from him on her cell.

I miss you, it read. Call me.

Right. First thing in the morning. Right after her bagel.

"Look, Lizzie, I'm not going to tell you what to do. You're right. I wasn't there. I'm not you, and you're not me. I just want to make sure you're not trying to hold on to this guy because of some mistaken sense of wanting to succeed at everything you try your hand at."

That was a new one.

Okay, so she was driven in her career. But was Tabby right in suggesting she applied that same ambition to her personal life?

Then again, Gauge was so unlike the men she usually dated as to be an aberration.

Which made her double think her options all the more.

Where did she hope a relationship with him might take her?

Well, for one thing, she was entertaining the thought of children.

She drew her knees up to her chest, wondering if she should turn on a light or restart the CD player or turn on the television. Instead she considered that last thought.

Yes, she admitted, for the first time in a long time she could see herself in the role of mother. Could envision lazy Sundays spent around the house, Gauge teaching them music, her fixing breakfast, all of them lounging on her and Gauge's bed reading the Sunday comics.

She'd really never fantasized about anything like that before. Her future with Jerry, when she'd thought about it, had been filled with investments and European vacations, boat purchases and expensive cars and clothes and nights at the opera. Children, when the subject presented itself, had included images of the nannies she'd need to look after them as she pursued her career and Jerry pursued his.

Strange that she'd never really viewed that as selfish before. So different from her own upbringing.

She grimaced. Speaking of her own upbringing, she really needed to get updated on what the family intended to do next Thursday for Christmas.

Did she love Gauge?

Now there was a question.

And, strangely enough, it was one she'd asked herself countless times over the past few days in the wake of Sunday's events. At first, she'd answered with an angry, unqualified no. But as time ticked ever ahead, she was coming to doubt her own quick judgment. She'd experienced a connection with him that she'd never felt before with another human being, much less a man. Had spent a full day of doing nothing but making love and had not felt one iota of guilt for wasting the time. She had not only listened to him talk about his past, but wanted to take away the pain so evident in his voice and absorb it into herself.

She'd once heard that true love meant putting the other person before yourself. And that the only way you could do that was if you loved yourself first.

Did she love herself?

And if she did love Gauge, what happened from there? Would he accept her love? Could he accept it? Could he let her in and let her love him even if he couldn't admit that he loved her, too?

So many ifs.

Which was part of the reason that she was growing more convinced that she did love him. Or was falling in love with him. Since she was beginning to think that she'd never really experienced the emotions before—except on the shallowest of levels—she couldn't begin to say. But the uncertainty of it felt like a thousand butterflies fluttering in her stomach, trying to get out.

She'd never felt so miserable in her life.

She'd never felt so euphoric.

Wasn't that how love was described?

She stared at the embers in the fireplace grate. She couldn't say for sure if she was in love with Gauge. But she did know that she wanted to love him.

She turned to look out the window again and saw the lights on in his apartment. Her heart skipped a beat.

He was home.

She tossed the throw to the other side of the couch and got up, determined to find out if he wanted to love her in return.

GAUGE STOOD at the window, staring out at Lizzie's house, much as he had over the past two nights. The place was dark. Not that he was surprised. He did find, however, that he was disappointed.

Hadn't he been the one to plan it that way? To avoid Lizzie at all costs? To be away when she returned from work? To come back after she had gone to bed?

Why, then, was he wishing she had left a light on?

"Gauge?"

He turned toward the female voice, so lost in his thoughts that he was almost startled by the appearance of Debbie, the waitress from the pub, sitting on the side of his bed.

Damn it all to hell, but he couldn't help remembering when Lizzie had sat the same way a scant week earlier.

Is that all it had been? A week? It felt like he'd known her a lifetime.

Debbie patted the mattress next to her. He grimaced, rubbing the back of his neck.

Inviting her back to his place had seemed like a good idea at the time. A decision made by his old friend Jack rather than him.

But that was a cop-out, wasn't it? In truth, he'd brought Debbie back here for one purpose, and one purpose only: to exorcise Lizzie from his mind and his life. And he knew that nothing would do that quicker than a roll in the hay with another woman.

Coward, a voice in the back of his mind whispered.

Who did he think he was kidding? All he was doing

was beating Lizzie to the punch. There wasn't a snow angel's chance in hell of anything between them working out. She was garden parties and career driven. He was bar crowds and happy if he had enough to see him through the next day.

Still, he couldn't help wishing that wasn't the case.

None of that changed the fact that Debbie was here and Lizzie was not.

"Gauge?" Debbie's voice held a thread of uncertainty.

Do it, he told himself. Go over there and take what she's offering. Forget about Lizzie. She deserves better than you.

He began walking in her direction. Debbie immediately relaxed and slid back on the bed, prepared to welcome him.

There was a brief knock on the door and then it opened inward.

"Thank God, I thought you'd never get home…"

Gauge froze, staring at Lizzie, who had just walked in, her words trailing off as she realized he wasn't alone.

She looked from him to Debbie then back again. Her sensual mouth worked around some sort of response, but nothing came out.

Then she turned and ran.

16

LIZZIE FELT as if her heart might beat straight out of her rib cage as she hurried from the apartment. She took the stairs two at a time, nearly slipping on the icy driveway, practically tripping over her own feet in her hurry to get out of there, to get away from Gauge, to banish the image of him leaning over the bed to kiss another woman.

She felt sick to her stomach, and was dreadfully afraid that the sob gathering at the back of her throat might erupt as she ran.

"Lizzie!"

She knew a moment of terror at the sound of Gauge calling for her, lending wings to her feet as she navigated the snowy path back to her house. She grabbed the back door handle and tugged, only to realize that she'd locked it when she'd left a few minutes earlier. She reached into her sweater pocket for her keys, desperate to lock herself inside where nothing and no one could ever hurt her again.

She finally worked the right key inside and ducked into the kitchen. She gasped when Gauge grabbed the door, preventing her from pulling it closed.

She turned and resumed running. She could find a room, lock herself inside. Somewhere, anywhere to hide herself away. To hide from him. To keep from showing him how very much he'd just hurt her.

She'd made it to the hall when he caught her around the waist.

She twisted to face him. "Don't you touch me! You've lost all rights to ever lay a hand on me again."

He ignored her pleas, holding her tight.

Lizzie pressed her open palms against his chest at the same time he released her. She stumbled backward, realized she was free and turned to run. Gauge reached out to steady her and she slapped at his arms, trading her balance for pure, angry need. She fell to the floor and he followed after her, his weight trapping her against the lush Oriental hall rug.

"Let…me…go!"

Lizzie twisted and turned, horrified that her cheeks were wet with tears. She couldn't believe she was doing what she was. Even in her darkest times with Jerry, she had never lost control of herself. Never demonstrated such raw, feral emotion.

Because she had never felt it.

"Shh," Gauge said, placing his hands on either side of her head as he fought to still her.

"Don't you tell me to be quiet! Damn you!"

She lashed out with her legs, trying to make him get off her. This couldn't be happening. Not to her. She was the one who always knew what she was doing, what she was getting into. And this…this was more than casual sex with just anybody. Somewhere down the line she had fallen in love with Gauge. Fully. Completely. Irrevocably.

And now he knew that.

Humiliation landed squarely on top of the maelstrom of emotions rushing through her body.

As hard as she fought, he calmly held her in place, not physically hurting her, but not letting her go, either.

Finally, the rage slowly seeped from her body, leaving her a heaving mass of pain and regret.

"I can't believe I let you do this to me. I can't believe I did this to myself."

Gauge pressed the side of his head against hers. She could feel his breath against her ear. "What did you do, Lizzie?" he whispered, his own voice rough with emotion.

She wriggled until he was forced to look into her face. "Why?" she asked. "Why did you do that? Why when…"

He searched her eyes. In his, she saw the same grab bag of emotions roiling inside her.

But that couldn't be. He didn't care about her. If he did, he would never have taken another woman back to his place. Another woman he'd planned to sleep with in the same spot he'd seduced her a week ago.

Only he hadn't seduced her, had he? She'd seduced him. She'd been dumb enough to think that a wild night of sex with the guitar-playing tenant would help distract her from her breakup with Jerry.

Stupid her.

"Why won't you let me love you?" she whispered.

GAUGE FELT as though she'd jabbed her fingers through his chest and ripped his heart clean out at her softly spoken words. Her eyes glistened like blue diamonds. Her cheeks were red and damp. And even though she'd settled down some, her body still heaved, bursting with pain and hatred and anger.

It seemed odd that the word *love* could fit into the equation anywhere. But in that instant, he knew that it was true. Lizzie did love him.

And, shocking as it was to admit, he knew that he was falling for her.

"Why?" she said again.

Gauge winced as if she'd shouted instead of whispered. He closed his eyes and smoothed her soft hair back from her face over and over again, his hands trembling, his stomach feeling like the years of whiskey he'd fed it had just rotted it.

He realized they were still on the floor, that he held her trapped against a rug. But he couldn't seem to force himself off her. He knew a need so strong to keep her there, a fear that if he let her up, she might never be in his arms again.

"This is so crazy," she said, sniffing harshly, as if equal parts sad and determined to regain control over herself. "I didn't believe it, either. Not completely. Not until this instant." She drew in a deep breath. "God, I never knew I could hurt this much."

Gauge rubbed his thumb against her bottom lip. "Shh," he said, not wanting to put words to the moment, to the feelings.

"I mean, I barely know you. How could I have fallen for you in such a short time? How can seeing you with another woman make me feel like I want to die?"

Gauge opened his eyes, viewing the truth in her face. A face made more beautiful in that one moment than it had ever been.

Had he ever been loved in this way? Had he ever loved in this way? Was this even love, this obsessive, possessive need that pressed on him, inside and out?

"I thought I knew love," she said, shaking her head. "But I didn't. Not really."

Gauge didn't want to hear any more. Couldn't bear to. So he did the only thing he knew would stop her.

He kissed her.

LIZZIE FOUGHT the gesture. She turned her head from side to side, not wanting to feel anything for him. She fought with everything that she had against the tidal wave of emotion threatening to undo her. Gauge merely kissed her harder, demanding access to her mouth, pressing his body insistently against hers. He worked a knee between hers and forced her thighs open, settled himself against her even as he sought access to her mouth.

No! her mind cried.

Yes! her heart responded.

She finally gave in and opened her mouth to him, bittersweet emotion filtering over her. How could she go from pain to pleasure within a heartbeat?

Gauge kissed her hard, his breathing coming in rapid gasps as he reached for the front of her blouse. Lizzie could taste the whiskey on his tongue. Could feel the persistent hardness of his erection between her legs. She helped him open her blouse and he nuzzled her breasts through the fabric of her bra before half-tearing it off so he could pull a nipple deep into his mouth.

She gasped, her back coming up off the rug as she tore at the catch of his jeans. He followed suit, stripping her of her pants. Within moments they were joined. Nothing between them. No condom. No inhibitions. Only wild, needy, bittersweet sex.

Lizzie moaned, grabbing his backside roughly as he thrust into her. She hooked her feet around his calves and kissed him hungrily, wet, openmouthed kisses that bruised her lips. He sank into her and she met him thrust for thrust until the world exploded into vivid shades of red.

Gauge rolled off her. They both lay out of breath, staring at the chandelier hanging from the foyer ceiling above them.

Lizzie felt strangely numb.

Gauge slid his fingers under hers and held her hand. She held his back.

This was it, she thought. This was the point where they decided what happened. Either they went on from here, tried to heal the wounds of the night and build on what they had. Or this was where they parted ways.

She didn't know which she wanted. Couldn't say. Half of her wanted him so desperately to stay, it scared her.

The other…well, the other half was scared of the power of that emotion.

So she lay there and allowed Gauge to make the decision.

When, long minutes later, he sat up, fixed his jeans and then got to his feet, she knew what his decision would be. And she was helpless to stop him.

She lay there, prone, as his boots sounded against the marble tile, then the tile of the kitchen, and he let himself out of the back door.

17

GAUGE SHOVED his things into his duffel. His apartment
had been empty when he returned, saving him the trouble of telling the waitress to go home. All he knew was
a need, a burning desire to get the hell out of there as
fast as he could.

"The Gauge men are known for itchy feet," his father
had once told him during a three-day bender. "They
can't stay in one place for too long before the need to
roam sends them on to the next place."

Gauge had never believed him. Had always thought
that his father had left a town behind in exchange for
the next one because it was the easy thing to do.

But his own decision to leave had to be the most difficult thing he'd ever done. Harder still than leaving last
February after his friendship with Nina and Kevin had
disintegrated.

"Why won't you let me love you?"

Lizzie's tearful words just minutes ago tore at his
soul. He fell back against the wall, causing a small shelf
to slant, dumping a potted plant onto the floor.

Not that he noticed. His heart was beating a million

miles a minute, his mouth was dry, and he wanted nothing more than to go across the yard and spend the next fifty years in that bed with Lizzie Gilbred.

Which was exactly the reason he couldn't.

He was damaged goods. He knew that. Had always known that. He had too much of his father in him not to be. Give him a good thing, and he would surely turn it bad sooner or later. This time it had just happened sooner rather than later.

No. He had to leave. For Lizzie's sake.

Liar.

The word echoed through his brain.

What was he supposed to do? He couldn't stand to remember the heart-wrenching pain on her face earlier when she'd spotted the waitress sitting on his bed, the same spot she'd been just a short time ago. He'd hurt her. Perhaps beyond repair.

But even if he could repair things, would he?

To what end?

He'd never been one to subscribe to or aspire to the Great American Dream. He'd taken over the music shop on a whim when he started spending copious amounts of time there while passing through Fantasy. The old man who'd owned it turned out to be a kindred spirit. Albeit one who had changed his own life. After ten years out on the road traveling from gig to gig when he was younger, he'd met the woman who would become his wife in Fantasy and they'd gone on to have three kids.

At first, Gauge hadn't understood his fascination

with the man. Sure, he was a talented artist. And he'd never been much for judging others on their decisions, probably because he didn't want to be judged on his. But Colin Murphy…well, he'd intrigued Gauge.

Was it possible to change?

Then the old man had died and deeded his shop to Gauge. A surprise considering his wife and three children were still alive. But the family—who happened to be well-off because Murphy's wife was a physician and the children had careers and families of their own—had been pleased, understanding that Gauge had come to mean a lot to Murphy.

Not even Gauge had realized how fond Murphy had been of him until he'd been given the shop.

He liked to tell himself that the reason he'd accepted the incredible gift was to honor Colin Murphy. But while that was true to a certain extent, it wasn't the whole truth. He'd accepted it because somewhere deep down, he'd wondered if he himself could change. Forge a different path than the one his father had shown him.

That decision had snowballed into a series of others he might never have made if not for Colin's gift, further fueling his desire for change. He'd joined forces with Nina and Kevin to create BMC and…well, after what had happened with Lizzie, he now knew that his father's blood ran deeper than he'd acknowledged before.

If there was one thing he was coming to understand, it was that you couldn't change blood. It would always tell.

The telephone began ringing again. He ignored it as he snapped out of his reverie and continued packing.

Minutes later he heard footfalls on the steps outside his apartment. They seemed to hesitate a moment, then there was a brief knock on his door and it opened inward.

Lizzie stood there, coatless, her face pale, her eyes still smeared with pain, her arms wrapped around her body.

He turned and put the last of his things in his bag. He walked to the table, avoiding her gaze, and stared at an envelope on the table. He picked it up and put it in the bag.

"There's been a fire," she said quietly. "It's BMC."

FLASHING LIGHTS BRIGHTENED the night sky, but they were no match for the flames that licked out of the upper windows of the building that housed BMC. Fire trucks were positioned at different angles in the parking lot, one from a bordering city, another a volunteer engine, all working to knock down the fire that looked to be consuming the bookstore/music center/café whole.

Gauge brought his car to a squealing stop just inside the parking lot and climbed out, barely remembering to shut off the engine and take the keys from the ignition. He rushed toward the building, his heart thundering in his chest.

A firefighter caught him before he could cross the line created by the trucks. "Sir, you need to keep back and let us work."

"I've got to get inside!" he shouted.

Please let Nina and Kevin be safe, he silently prayed. Let them have been at home.

"Gauge!"

He turned toward the familiar male voice. Kevin. He stood across the parking lot, a crying Nina in his arms.

Thank God.

Gauge hurried toward them.

"Was anyone hurt?" was his first question as he eyed his friends, looking for apparent injuries.

"No. Everyone's safe. The place was securely locked down for the night."

Nina looked pale. "It was the oven, I know it was." She squeezed her eyes shut. "The replacement is…was due to be delivered tomorrow."

Assured that everyone was all right, Gauge turned back toward the store. The firefighters appeared to be concentrating on keeping the fire from spreading to neighboring establishments. The absence of wind helped, but the cold temperatures did not.

"Nina, I want you to let Heidi take you home," Kevin said. And for the first time Gauge noticed Nina's friend and former employee standing a few feet away.

"But I don't want to go home by myself. Not with our lives going up in smoke."

Gauge watched as Kevin gently touched his wife's pretty face. "Not our lives, baby. Our business. That can be rebuilt."

"But—"

"Come on," Heidi agreed, apparently sensing the same thing Gauge did: that Kevin had something to say to him. And he didn't want to do it with Nina present.

Finally, Nina went with Heidi, looking over her

shoulder as she did. Kevin waited until the two women were out of sight before he lit into Gauge.

"What in the hell did you do?" he demanded.

LIZZIE SAT on the floor of the apartment that had been Gauge's. Only it really hadn't been his beyond his name on the lease, had it? He'd never made it his home. Not if he could clear out of there in five minutes flat and not leave a single thing behind beyond the bottle of Jack Daniel's on the table.

She leaned her back against the wall, making out shapes in the dark. The chairs. The kitchen counter. The bed.

She swallowed hard, crowding her fingers through her hair, surprised she still had tears to cry.

What was that saying? You never knew what you had until it was gone?

Or, rather, after you'd chased it away?

She gave a humorless laugh. First she'd chased Gauge away after what he'd done with Jerry the other day. Then today he'd chased her away.

And that's what he'd done, wasn't it? Just as she'd desperately been looking for a way to ease the pain of her breakup with Jerry and found it in Gauge's bed, he'd been looking for a final break from her by inviting a woman back to his place, where he'd known she'd be sure to see her. If not tonight, then in the morning when the woman left.

Or, maybe not. Maybe she was giving herself far too much credit. Maybe Gauge didn't feel for her what she felt for him, and tonight had just been another night to him.

She remembered the trembling way he'd held her at her place just a short time ago, refusing to let her go, his face mirroring her anguish, and couldn't bring herself to believe it.

Why, then, the betrayal?

It was almost funny, really. It wasn't so long ago that she'd thought Jerry was the man for her. Had been devastated when he'd dumped her...not once, but twice. But now...

Well, now she recognized her feelings in the wake of Jerry's betrayal as pride. The first time, she'd been unable to see beyond what looked good on paper. Jerry and her, a successful marriage to go with their successful independent careers. She had known there was no love between them. At least not true love.

But she wasn't completely to blame. If only because she'd had no idea what true love entailed. What it demanded.

She hurt in ways that surpassed the physical. Her entire body seemed to throb. Her heart seemed to shiver, trying to hide from the pain that ricocheted through her. Tomorrow loomed bleak and meaningless, a gaping black hole to fill with...with what?

If told two weeks ago that it would be sexy musician Patrick Gauge who would steal her soul, show her what love truly was, she'd have laughed at the messenger.

But there you had it. No matter what arguments she

tried to use against it, how hard she battled against it, there was no ignoring or denying the truth. And the truth was that she loved Patrick Gauge. Despite his flaws. Despite his betrayal. Merely being with him made her feel whole and no longer alone in the world.

She only wished she had figured that out before it was too late.

GAUGE STUMBLED back a couple of steps, losing his balance when Kevin pushed him.

"What in the hell did you do?" Kevin demanded, advancing on him like a man gone mad.

"What are you talking about?"

He blinked at his partner and one-time best friend, trying to figure out the way his mind was working.

"The fire!" Kevin shouted. "Did you want out of our partnership that badly?"

"What?" Gauge's response was quiet as he digested his words.

Was Kevin accusing him of having set the fire? Of being responsible for the chaos being played out behind him?

Both his friend's anger and physical shove had knocked him off-kilter earlier, but now he found his footing and stared him down.

"Well, now, that's a new one," he said darkly. "Now you're accusing me of arson?"

Kevin advanced on him. Gauge held his ground, daring him to hit him. Not so Kevin could unleash his emotions at Gauge for having slept with Nina, but so

Gauge would be justified in hitting him back. Of giving outlet to his own unresolved emotions for Lizzie that were crowding his chest, leaving him little more than a walking bag of hormones and confusion.

"Tell me you didn't do it," Kevin demanded. "Tell me you didn't destroy BMC so that you could leave here once and for all."

Gauge leaned forward, putting them almost nose-to-nose. "I didn't set that damn fire, Kevin. So you'd better back off or else I won't be held responsible for my actions."

"What, are you going to hit me, Gauge? Go ahead. Because this time I won't be the one who holds back."

"I'd love nothing better than to sock you in the mouth just now, you smug bastard. But I won't. No. Not this time. Not so you can come out smelling like the rose you always do."

He was surprised by the caustic words but couldn't stop them.

"I did not set that fire," he repeated. "I can't believe you would even think that."

"What do you want me to think? You don't want to be involved in the running of the business. You don't cash the checks. Then overnight the place goes up in smoke? It's all a little too neat for me. The place burns down, you get a substantial little check to add to your pile, and you're free of BMC, of us and this town. Isn't that what you came back for, Gauge? To find a way to finally cut the ties you have here?"

He didn't know what to say, so he didn't say anything. There was a logic to Kevin's thinking that was a little eerie, because it was plausible.

"Admit it, Gauge, you're a liar and a cheat. You excuse yourself for doing things that someone else wouldn't do. Maybe you have good reasons for it. Maybe you don't. I can't say as I care anymore. Because now you'll be judged solely on your actions."

"Actions I didn't take."

Kevin held up his hand. "I said I don't care." He exhaled a long breath, looking a little more under control but no less dangerous. "Why do you think every other person in this town does the right thing, Gauge? You think it's because it's the way they were raised, or because it's easy? No. Making the right decision sometimes is the hardest thing you can do. But in the end it's up to you, as an individual, to make that decision. To weather that hardship.

"What, did you think that you could come here and have everything just drop into your lap? This perfect life? Well, I'm sorry to tell you, pal, you don't get it just because you open yourself up for it. You have to earn it. That's right, I said earn it. Not because you were dealt a crappy hand in life. Poor you. Get over yourself. Because that's just not going to fly anymore. Not with me. Not with my wife. Not with my family—the one you've tried to destroy."

"I didn't set the goddamn fire."

"I'm not talking about that."

No, he was talking about everything. And that "everything" explained why Kevin would think he was behind the fire. It stretched back to when he'd chosen to sleep with Nina. To put selfish need above the greater good. To do what was wrong instead of right.

He'd told himself that it had been hard to do what he had. But in truth, it had been easy.

It would have been much harder to have done the right thing.

The thought of what might have happened had he pushed Nina away that night, where he might be, where they as friends might be, knocked him back on his feet more forcibly than any shove Kevin could give him.

And he knew that he'd finally screwed this up beyond recovery.

He stalked to his car, grabbed something from his duffel and then went to stand before Kevin again. He held out the white envelope that had been on his table, the last thing he'd taken from his apartment.

"Go ahead. Take it."

Kevin did, holding it out as if he didn't know what to make of it.

"Those are papers signing over my third of BMC to you and Nina for one dollar."

He'd had the legal documents drawn up two days ago, after things had gone south with Lizzie. He figured it would give them all a clean slate to start over.

"And I know you don't believe this but…"

The end of the sentence seemed helplessly lodged in his throat. Maybe because it included a word he'd never said before, much less felt.

"I'm sorry."

He turned to leave. Not just the conversation or the parking lot or Lizzie…but Fantasy. For good.

18

SECONDS MELTED into minutes, minutes into hours, until two days later, without knowing that's where he was heading, or that his destination actually lay there, Gauge ended his journey in a dusty town in Arizona. A place familiar to him because he'd passed through years ago with his father.

He'd seen many towns in his travels. Some changed over the years, others seemed to be frozen in perpetuity, as if they were some sort of time capsule of what life might have looked like in the nineteen-fifties. Dirt roads on which modern cars kicked up red dirt; storefronts that still bore the same tin signs from that era, hanging from metal hooks, swaying in the dry, light wind.

Gauge had parked his car in a lot he remembered from long ago. The old roadhouse was set back from the two-lane road, the Closed sign turned, no indication of life when just a few short hours before it would have been teeming with people who might have driven over thirty miles for a night out, pickup trucks choking the gravel he now stood on.

He stared at the brightening eastern horizon, a haze

of purple. He wore only his T-shirt and jeans and boots, having shed layers of clothing the farther south he drove. He'd slept when he'd had little choice but to sleep, eaten when his body forced him, and driven the rest of the time, the car's worn tires taking him farther and farther away from Fantasy, Michigan.

Now he felt as if he'd stepped off the edge of the earth, having gone from winter snow to summer warm.

He wondered what Lizzie was doing. Considering the time difference, she was probably at work, striving to return to normalcy. Hiding her pain away.

He opened his car door and climbed back inside, within minutes pulling up to a nearby motel he'd stayed at with his father. He paid the man at the front desk and took the key, letting himself into a small bungalow at the end of a ramshackle row. The room smelled of cigarette smoke and booze and old carpeting. He dropped the key onto the small table inside the door and then went out to get his things. It didn't take him more than a few minutes to make the room home for however long he needed it.

He glanced at the bed, but even though his eyelids scraped against his eyes like sandpaper every time he blinked, he knew he wouldn't be able to go to sleep.

Instead, he grabbed his guitar and stepped through the back door that opened onto a makeshift patio of old bricks, desert weeds poking through the cracks. He sat down on the rusted metal chair there and pulled his guitar onto his knee. He closed his eyes and took in a deep breath of the dry, desert air, feeling the sun against his face rather than seeing it rise as the fingers of his left hand ran over the strings, strumming with the thumb and index finger of his right hand, even though he always carried a pick in his pocket.

He remembered the first time he could play a song on his own without looking at his hands. He'd been about nine and had been left in a random motel room by himself for the night, trusting that his father would be back at some point the next morning. He'd sat on the edge of the walk outside the room, his feet on the parking-lot asphalt, feeling his away around the song without the benefit of sight, trusting that his hands knew the way. They had. And from then on, he and his guitar had become best friends, conversing in a way that he'd never really learned how to with others.

As he played, images filled his mind. Of his father sitting across the room from him on a chair, smiling his grizzled grin as he smoked a cigarette, listening to Gauge play. Of the face of the woman who'd turned him into a man, and nearly every woman he'd found pleasure with since. Of Nina and Kevin and him laughing around the fireplace at BMC.

Of Lizzie's golden blond hair spread across his chest as she curved against his side like a sexy she-cat, smiling up at him in provocative invitation and, yes, love.

He also saw the hurt shine in her beautiful blue eyes as he'd held her down.

"Why won't you let me love you?"

Her words had been spoken so softly he nearly hadn't heard them.

Nina's smile followed on the heels of the memory, the morning they'd talked things out at the café, the last time he'd ever visit the place that had been a fixture in his life for three years.

"Admit it, Nina," he'd said. "In your heart of hearts, you knew that Kevin was the mystery man. Yet you slept with me anyway…."

He'd feared she would run away from the question. As a married woman, deny that she'd harbored feelings for another man not her husband. A husband who had at one time been Gauge's best friend, too.

But she hadn't. She'd looked down at her coffee cup, taking her time.

"I've thought about that night often," she'd finally said. "And, yes, I have come to admit to myself that when I came to you, I did so knowing full well that you might not be the man I'd been with before." She'd bitten her bottom lip. "But I had to know, Gauge. I had to know if there was a chance between us. Had to know if it would be as good between us as it was between Kevin and me."

"And was it?"

She'd swallowed hard but steadfastly held his gaze. "It was."

Gauge had known a satisfaction then that he'd felt instantly guilty about.

"But something was missing."

Love.

He'd known that's what she was going to say before she even said it. Because by then he was already falling in love with Lizzie. And it was only then that he'd recognized what he felt for Nina hadn't been the type of emotion that built relationships strong enough to weather whatever storm came their way. Not like the bond between Nina and Kevin, who had not only survived Gauge's ultimate act of betrayal, but had blossomed in spite—and, yes, perhaps even because—of it.

That's when Gauge had to confront the fact that he'd slept with Nina, claimed her physically, because of some desire of his own to win a competition that had started the instant the three of them quit being friends, and Nina and Kevin had become lovers. A battle of wills on a primitive level he wasn't entirely sure he understood, although he now recognized the drive to do so only too well.

Kevin's final words echoed through his mind: "Making the right decision sometimes is the hardest thing you can do. But in the end it's up to you to make that decision… What, did you think that you could come here and have everything just drop into your lap? This perfect life? Well, I'm sorry to tell you, pal, you don't get it just because you open yourself up for it. You have to earn it…."

Gauge hadn't realized that his hands had increased the pace, moving from a soothing piece to a hard, quick tempo, his fingers flying over the frets, his thumb strumming like there was no tomorrow. And there wasn't, was there? At least not a tomorrow with which he was familiar.

He finished the song with a final, almost violent strum and rested his hands against the body of the still vibrating instrument, his heart beating heavily in his chest, his breathing labored, the throbbing in his temples growing into a full-blown ache.

But nothing that matched the ache in his heart….

"So ARE YOU GOING to buy it, or are you just going to stand there looking at it all day?" Annie asked.

Lizzie blinked her younger sister into focus, her hand still grasping the black cotton T-shirt that read, Got Blues? and featured a drawing of an electric guitar. She and her sister had been passing the store in the mall and she'd wandered in without saying anything, leaving her sister to walk past two more stores before she figured out that Lizzie was no longer with her.

Now Annie stood with her arms crossed, staring at her sister, the bags hanging from her hands making it hard to see her as much of a threat.

Lizzie forced herself to release the T-shirt. But rather than follow her sister outside the store, she instead headed over to the store counter, looking at jewelry made of musical instruments, as well as plaques.

"God, that's so tacky," Annie said, eyeing a pair of earrings made out of amber-colored guitar picks.

Lizzie figured it was a good thing that her sister didn't know anything about her brief tryst with Gauge or else she'd probably find that highly tacky, as well.

"What's going on with you?" Annie asked, looking at her a little too closely. "Beyond a CD here and there, you've never showed an interest in music."

Lizzie picked up an acoustic guitar from a stand,

running her hand over the lacquered front. "Yes, well, maybe I'm thinking about taking it up."

"Well, at least choose something worthwhile. Like piano. Or if you're set on a stringed instrument, a harp."

Lizzie ignored her.

She couldn't say exactly what it was, but she felt somehow…more at ease in the store. She felt better than she had in the past five days since Gauge left. She kept waiting for the ache to lessen, for her heart to go back to beating normally, her eyes to close at night. Instead, the opposite seemed to be happening. The more time that passed, the more she seemed to think about him. About what could have been and how well they'd suited each other.

For the first time in her life, she'd met a man and didn't care whether or not he had a stock portfolio, or if he wore the right clothes or drove the right car. And while she'd convinced herself at the time that it had only been about sex, somewhere down the line she'd come to care about Gauge in a way that seemed insane.

He made her feel…like a woman.

Since the night she'd climbed into Gauge's bed, she'd become aware of herself in ways she hadn't imagined before. She'd always known she was as capable as a man in the business world, but in life…well, she found that she wanted to make Gauge breakfast in bed. Wanted to lick syrup off his body. Wanted to look sexy for him.

Of course, now that she'd realized the impact he'd had on her, she wouldn't be able to take full advantage of the changes he'd wrought in her. At least not in the sexual sense. But given the way she felt more in touch with herself as a woman, she craved more of a connection with everyone around her, an almost nurturing need for closeness. Perhaps not all was lost, she thought.

"Come on," Annie prodded her. "We're going to be late."

It was the Sunday night before Christmas and they were going to help their mother make holiday cookies.

She put the guitar down and allowed her sister to lead her out of the shop.

BEFORE LIZZIE KNEW IT, she was sitting at the kitchen table at her parents' house, her shirtsleeves rolled up, wearing her father's Kiss The Cook apron and stirring a fresh batch of frosting. Her sister had gone into the other room to take a call from her husband, and Lizzie and her mother were working in companionable silence. Her father was around somewhere, popping up every now and again to stick his finger in the icing.

Lizzie couldn't help thinking that it looked as if her parents had returned to normal. But at this point, she'd given up hoping.

"You're awfully quiet," her mother said as she sprinkled red sugar glitter onto a batch of freshly baked chocolate-mint cookies.

"Hmm?" Lizzie looked up. "Oh. Yes." She smiled as she pushed her hair back from her face. "I could say the same of you."

"Yes. I suppose you could."

They fell silent again. Every now and again they heard Annie raise her voice from the next room.

"I give her five minutes before she's out the door to go home to take care of whatever emergency popped up," her mother said.

"I give her three."

They were both wrong. Within a minute, Annie slammed the cordless back into the wall holder and sighed as she took off her apron. Hers read, If You Want Breakfast In Bed, Sleep In The Kitchen.

"Kid crisis. He can't find Jasmine, and Mason's having a conniption. I've got to go."

"Sounds like normal kid stuff to me," Bonnie said.

"Yes, well, my darling husband insists he's about to go insane and is begging me to come home now."

Lizzie shared a glance with her mother.

"We're almost done, anyway, right?" Annie said, giving her mother a kiss on the cheek and crossing to hug Lizzie. "I won't be missed."

"No, but you'll miss this," Bonnie said. "Don't forget to take a plate with you. If anything's guaranteed to make Jaz come out of hiding, and Mason to stop crying, it's a batch of the Gilbreds' annual Christmas cookies."

Annie smiled as she prepared a plate and then waved at them on her way out the door.

"And she actually wants another one?" Lizzie asked.

Her mother shrugged. "She's a better mother than I ever was."

"How can you say that? Don't get me wrong, I adore

my niece and nephew, but sometimes I want to check the back of their heads for a six-six-six tattoo."

Bonnie laughed. "God, I was an awful mother."

"You were not."

"Sure I was. I can't remember a time when I didn't stay awake nights terrified I was scarring you kids for life."

"I thought that came with parenthood."

"Yes, I suppose it does. To a certain extent, but…"

She seemed lost in her thoughts and Lizzie concentrated on frosting the rest of the cookies in front of her.

"Do you think you're a good wife?" Lizzie surprised herself by asking.

Bonnie stared at her.

"What? It's a fair question."

If she had her own personal agenda for asking, she wasn't going to say. While a part of her wished that she'd told her family about Gauge, another was glad she hadn't. For all they knew, she was still dating Jerry.

"I was the absolute worst wife imaginable," Bonnie said quietly, stressing the word *was*. She went to remove a tray of cookies from the oven. "What does that mean, anyway? What is a wife's job? To make her husband happy? And what is a husband's job? To make his wife happy?" She snorted indelicately.

Lizzie watched her father sneak up behind her mother and snatch one of the cookies just out of the oven, putting his finger to his lips to tell Lizzie not to say anything. He tossed the hot cookie from hand to hand, trying to cool it, and then ducked out of the room again to go back to whatever he was doing.

Lizzie shook her head. "I don't know. I suppose it once meant that a husband was supposed to take care of the family financially. And the wife was supposed to keep the house running."

Her mother dropped her arms to her sides. "Roles. I've always hated prescribed roles."

"But you've always been a great wife and mother."

"Whatever." She fell silent for a few moments. Lizzie stepped to the kitchen island to transfer the warm cookies to cooling racks and peeked inside the oven to make sure everything was progressing as it should.

"You know, the only reason I ever married your father was because I was pregnant with you."

Lizzie experienced a moment of shock. "No. No, I, um, didn't know."

"That's not to say that I don't love your father. Or that we haven't had a good life together."

Lizzie returned to her side of the table, resisting the urge to guide the conversation.

"I've never been a traditional kind of girl." Bonnie frowned as she looked around her. "Holidays and my children aside."

"Define traditional?"

Bonnie blinked up at her. "For one, I never wanted to be married. Never thought a piece of paper mattered when it comes to emotional unions." She placed her hands on the table and leaned forward. "It's like ownership papers. And it wreaks terrible havoc on a relationship."

"Mom…why do you love Dad?"

That seemed to catch her up short. "Why? Well, that's simple. He balances me. Completes me."

Bonnie smiled, as if to herself.

"Now your dad…he's the traditional one. If I'd fallen in love with anyone else, I could very easily be making these cookies with you in a tent somewhere."

"Tent?"

"Sure. Why not? It's your father who wants all the traditional trappings. The house. The cottage at the lake." She gave Lizzie a sidelong gaze. "The marriage."

She walked two trays of cookies into the dining room and then came back, wiping her hands on her apron, which read, Some Like It Spicy.

"Expectations and assumptions can sink a relationship faster than you can burn cookies," her mother said, then glanced over her shoulder. "Speaking of which…"

"They're fine. I just checked."

Bonnie looked thoughtful.

"So," Lizzie said. "You're really going to go through with this divorce thing then…?"

Bonnie looked surprised. "Of course I am. There's no question of that."

Lizzie felt suddenly sad.

"Don't look so down in the mouth. As far as you kids are concerned, nothing's going to change."

"What? How can they not change? Our mother is divorcing our father."

Bonnie smiled mischievously. "Yes, but your mother and father are not splitting up."

To Lizzie, that made absolutely no sense at all.

She braced herself for her mother's explanation.

19

MUCH LATER that night, Lizzie sat in her own kitchen, sipping an Irish coffee and thinking about the Bonnie Gilbred take on divorce.

"Labels, roles, expectations…what a bunch of malarkey. I'm tired of making joint decisions, of worrying I'm not living up to a standard others set. In this case, your father. And he's not the only one to blame. I do the same thing. Before you know it, you're taking each other for granted. Or falling short of the mark so often your self-esteem doesn't just take a hit, you wake up one morning and it's gone altogether."

So her mother's solution to the problem was that they should get a divorce. No longer would she be beholden to some archaic way of thinking, but a woman free to make decisions as she saw fit. A woman who wasn't part of a pair, but an individual who could walk away with no ties if she wanted.

As a result, she explained, her father would appreciate her more. And she would appreciate him. Enjoy him.

"Our sex life hasn't been this good since you guys were kids."

Lizzie hadn't wanted to travel any further on that particular train of thought, although she had to admit that her mother's take on marriage had its own kind of twisted logic.

Which, of course, brought her thoughts back to Gauge.

She looked through the kitchen window at the garage apartment, dark and cold. Everything remained exactly the way Gauge had left it, down to the sleep-rumpled bedding. Of course, he'd been gone less than a week, and his lease didn't end until the end of February, but she knew that he wouldn't be returning.

She sipped her coffee, the Irish cream warming her.

Given how she felt about Gauge now, why hadn't she seen him as a threat to her freedom, to her heart, when she originally crossed the driveway and climbed the steps to his apartment? Was it because he was a transient musician and didn't fit any of her previous qualifications for the type of man she thought she'd spend the rest of her life with?

"He balances me," were her mother's words.

Lizzie recognized that to be true. Where her mother was flighty and fiercely independent, her father had always been the rock. Every aspect of their lives reflected that. Her father was a builder, using solid materials to make long-lasting structures that could weather the worst storms.

Her mother was going to be a flight attendant.

She shook her head, still having trouble wrapping her brain around that one.

She supposed that was because she was so much

like her father. Or, rather, his type. Driven. Career oriented. Ambitious.

Could it be that opposites attracted for a reason? Could Gauge be the yin to her yang? The other side of the seesaw? Could he be the home to her house?

And on the flip side, could she be the rock he clung to in a storm? The one who took care of the financial end, not because she had to, but because she wanted to, so he could be a guitar player, free to choose which gigs he took.

Of course, all this was speculation. What remained was that the physical pain she'd experienced upon his departure felt like a lingering wound that she feared might never heal.

So if that was the case, and she was in love with him, did any of the other stuff really matter? Should she, like her mother, do something strictly because it felt good?

She recalled the day she and Gauge spent in bed. Without qualification, it remained the single most sublime time of her life. And he, and only he, had given that to her.

She glanced around her house. Stuff. Stuff she liked, but in the end, just stuff. She could do without it if she had to.

Gauge…

She caught her breath, her heart hurting all over again at the thought that odds were she was going to have to live without him.

Although it was after eleven on a Sunday night, Lizzie picked up the phone and dialed a number.

"Hello?" Her ex-almost-sister-in-law Heidi answered her cell on the fifth ring.

"I need you to tell me where Gauge might have gone…"

WHEN GAUGE WASN'T THINKING about Lizzie, he was dreaming about her. When he wasn't dreaming about her, he was thinking about her. Every moment of every day.

He'd never known any woman to take a hold of his soul and his sanity like this. All he wanted to do was touch her. To make love to her. To make her smile, make her laugh. Everything else came a distant second. And time and distance was doing nothing to change that.

He crossed his arms as he leaned against his dusty old car, squinting against the setting winter sun on the desert horizon. He'd spent his life playing the blues. While he understood the concept of existential blues, he really hadn't gotten the ones about love. Oh, he'd thought he had. But it wasn't until he'd surrendered his heart to Lizzie, and betrayed her love, that he truly understood the meaning of singing the blues.

A rusty pickup kicked up dust on the road in the distance. He cupped his hand over his eyes to watch it approach. It was just after five, the time the man he wanted to see would return home from work. He glanced at the old two-bedroom trailer some hundred yards away, noticing the way the curtains fluttered at the window. It wasn't much, but it was obvious the family that lived there took pride in what they did have. The area around it was clean, everything well tended.

The truck slowed and pulled off the road onto the dirt area that served as the trailer's driveway. Gauge had parked there and stood waiting as the driver pulled to a stop and eyed him warily.

There wasn't much to connect the man before him with the boy he'd been when Gauge had last seen him. But there was enough of their father in him to recognize him as Gorge, his half brother.

"I don't know if you remember me, but I thought we might talk," Gauge said, squinting into the sunset and then back again.

"I know who you are." Gorge glanced at the trailer. The honey-skinned young woman Gauge had spoken to earlier appeared holding a toddler on her hip, her belly round with another child on the way.

Gauge thought for a minute that his half brother might tell him to come back some other time and continue on to his family. Instead, he waved at the woman, shut off his engine and climbed from the truck.

"Hey, man," he said, offering his hand. "How long you been out my way?"

Gauge welcomed the physical contact, patting the back of Gorge's hand with his other one and holding it still for a long moment as he searched his face.

He'd never tried to make any sort of contact with his father's other children. His brothers and sister. But he'd come to realize over the past couple of days that it was that need that had brought him here, to the one brother he had met.

What remained was whether Gorge would want anything to do with him now.

"I just got into town the night before last," he said, finally releasing his hand.

Gorge nodded. "Got a gig in town?"

"No. Just decided to drive down."

"Down? So you were up north then. Winters can get pretty bad up that way."

Gauge smiled at the congenial way Gorge spoke to him, automatically trying to put him at ease. "Yes. Yes, that they can." He gestured toward Gorge's soot-covered jeans and denim shirt. "You working the copper plant in Hayden?"

"Yeah." Gorge made to brush himself off. "Ever since we moved off San Carlos."

Gauge recognized the name of the Indian Reservation nearby. He had known Gorge was of mixed heritage, but hadn't known the origins of his mother. Was she Apache? Or was Gorge's wife?

"Good work?" he asked.

"Good enough."

Gauge nodded.

Since he wasn't all that clear on what he wanted beyond a chance to see the younger man, and know that he was doing well, he didn't quite know what to say.

And Gorge also appeared to have run out of small talk. He shifted his stance, scratching his head as he looked at his young wife again. "Look, I hope you're not here looking for money or anything—"

"No, no," Gauge said quickly, holding up his hands. "That's not it at all. I…"

He, what?

He'd thought about what he might say. About what they might talk about. But all of it seemed insignificant in the dimming light.

"I just wanted, you know, to come by to see that you were okay."

Gorge considered the dirt under his boots and then cocked his brow. "To give me money like the old man used to do when he came through town?"

Gauge grimaced. "No. I was looking for something more, maybe…"

To his surprise, Gorge merely nodded.

"You wanna come in for a beer or something, man? Meet the wife and the son?" He looked suddenly surprised. "Wow. I just realized that he's your nephew."

His nephew.

Gauge tried the word out as he looked toward the trailer and the woman and child that still waited.

Gorge must have taken his slow response as reluctance. "Hey, you know, you don't have to or anything."

"No, no." Gauge smiled. "I'd like to come meet your family…my nephew and sister-in-law. I'd like that a lot."

20

"YOU'RE GOING into the office on Christmas Eve?"

Annie's voice sounded incredulous over the phone.

"Yes. Along with nearly every other working citizen," Lizzie said. "At least until noon."

"That's sacrilegious."

Lizzie resisted giving an eye roll even though her sister couldn't see her.

"Isn't Roger going in?"

"Yes, but he's different."

"Different how? Because he's a man?"

It was hard to believe that her sister used to be one of the most in-demand ad execs in Toledo. Four years out of the professional workplace, four years locked in a house with toddlers would do that to a woman, she guessed.

"Never mind." Annie sighed, and Lizzie heard Mason crying. "Anyway, what time are you going to be at Mom and Dad's tonight?"

"I don't know. The usual time, I guess. Around eight or nine?"

"So late?"

"Why? What time were you planning on going over?"

"Around six or seven."

"That makes for a long night."

"That makes for a good time to get the kids to sleep in my old room so I can have a little bit of fun. You know, the adult kind that doesn't include sticky fingers and cranky demands."

Lizzie sighed as she rinsed out her coffee cup in the kitchen sink and then put it in the dishwasher. "I'm meeting Tabitha for a late lunch, then running a couple of errands. I suppose I can try to speed everything up so I can get there at around…seven." She opted for the later time rather than the earlier one.

"Great! On your way up, can you stop by Brieschkes and pick me up a bear claw?"

Lizzie's jaw dropped. "What about all the Christmas cookies?"

"I'm craving a bear claw."

Pregnant women and their cravings. Sometimes she thought her sister enjoyed being pregnant a little too much.

Well, at least she wasn't asking for her to stop at Krispy Kreme, which was a couple of miles in the opposite direction.

"Fine." She gave in.

"Buy three."

"You can only eat one."

"Yes, but I might want another one in the morning. And the other…is for backup."

"Fine," Lizzie said again. "Anything else?"

She'd meant the question to be sarcastic, but her sister appeared to be thinking about it. She was glad when Annie finally said, "No, that should about cover it."

"Great."

Lizzie looked at her watch. Almost eight-thirty. She was already running later than she intended.

"Look, sis, I've really got to go. Kiss the kids for me."

The doorbell rang. Lizzie craned her neck to stare into the hall as if she could tell who was outside just by looking at the door.

"Okay. Call me when you get off."

"Sure."

Lizzie pressed the disconnect button and put the phone down on the counter. The doorbell rang again.

"I'm coming, I'm coming."

Not an auspicious beginning to the holiday. She was already feeling rushed and harried.

She looked through the peephole to find one of those fantastic-looking UPS guys grinning at her, his teeth looking a little threatening given the fish-eye lens.

She hadn't ordered anything. Had she?

"Merry Christmas," he said as she opened the door.

"Same to you."

"If I can have you sign here."

Lizzie accepted the digital signing device as she looked at the three-by-two foot box he'd placed next to his feet. "Does it say where it's from?"

"It appears to be a personal delivery. From Arizona."

She didn't know anyone in Arizona.

She thought about investigating further before accepting, but curiosity got the better of her. If it ended up being intended for one of her neighbors, she'd simply deliver it herself.

"Thank you. Have a great holiday."

Lizzie accepted the package and distractedly wished him the same, closing the door again.

For long moments she stood in the foyer staring at the box, her heart beating a steady rhythm in her chest.

She really should be getting to work.

She really needed to open this box, a little voice argued.

For reasons she couldn't define, her palms felt damp and her throat thick. She opened the drawer in the hall table and withdrew the letter opener there, using it to slit open the tape on the top and sides of the box. She carefully laid it on the floor and then pulled open the flaps. Packing material. Lots of it. She reached in, hauling out Bubble Wrap and crumpled paper. A few moments later she stared at the item nestled inside, feeling as if her breath had been stolen from her.

She backed up until her heels met the bottom stair and then she sank down to sit on the steps, unable to believe what she was seeing.

It wasn't possible, was it? Of all the things she could have imagined receiving, this would have been the last.

Through misty eyes, she clicked open the protective case and took out an item she thought she'd never see again. Something so person specific, so magnificently unique. She handled it with the awe and respect and gratitude a curator might give a priceless work of art, carefully turning it over, tracing the scratches on the back with her fingertips.

Gauge's acoustic guitar.

"Wherever my guitar is, my heart is."

She remembered his words, spoken softly on the first night they spent together, before they'd begun their sexual journey.

She sat for long minutes holding it. Placing her hands where she imagined his might have lain, her touch warming the wood, feeling connected to him.

Reluctantly, she put the guitar back in the case and searched the box for a note. There was nothing. But she did know something important. It had come from Arizona.

Which meant that's where Gauge was.

Mixed emotions swirled through her. She was touched beyond description at the gift. Hurt that he wasn't there to give it to her himself.

Beyond all that, she was soul-stirringly aware that she hadn't seen the last of Patrick Gauge and that their love affair might not yet have reached its end.

THE NIGHT WAS QUIET. As it should be on Christmas Eve, he thought.

Gauge stood on the doorstep, tentative. A lot had happened over the past week. Much that he couldn't name. A good deal that he could.

He'd gotten to know his brother, had been accepted by his wife and embraced by his nephew, who didn't care what had gone before, or what existed between his father and this man, but judged him solely by his ability to give a belly tickle. It was something Gauge found he was quite proficient at, even though he had no prior experience. The sound of the boy's laughter had touched him in places he hadn't known existed. Places that he might not have been able to reach a short time before…before Lizzie opened them, made them accessible. Before she had made him take a new look at life and love and the future.

So in a roundabout way he had her to thank that he was now Uncle G to little Thomas, a honey-skinned boy Gorge had given their father's name.

"Looks like you're doing well for yourself," he'd said to Gorge a couple days into his visit when the two had been enjoying a beer outside after dinner, poking at a fire Gorge had started to chase off the desert chill of the early evening.

Gorge had shrugged, looking toward the trailer that was home, and probably thinking about the woman inside doing the dinner dishes, his son asleep in his crib in their bedroom, the baby due in a month.

"Not bad, considering. I'm saving to get us into a real home hopefully sometime next year. But until then, we're okay."

More than okay, they were a cohesive family unit. Happy. Loving. Affectionate. Gauge could see it in the way they touched, smiled and spoke. It was evident in their every move. And he envied them for how easy it seemed.

"Your mother…does she live nearby?"

"Yeah." Gorge pointed the bottle northeast. "On the rez."

"You're Apache, then."

"Half." Gorge grinned at him, likely realizing that Gauge would be one of the few people who would know that.

"I'm glad you've had solid family support. A home."

His brother leaned forward and looked at him. "Not so much as you would think. My mom married when I was three and went on to have three more children. I was always the odd man out." He looked into the fire, his thoughts far away, then glanced back at Gauge. "No. My home, my family is that woman in there. My wife. The mother of my children." He shook his head. "I know so long as we're together, so long as she loves me, then I'll have all I'll ever want in this world."

Gauge blinked now, slowly coming back to the present and the door he stood outside. He had more than a few regrets. Gorge was a wonderful man, strong and honest and hardworking. He wished he had made the effort to know before. But he supposed it was good enough that he was coming to know him now. And both men had vowed to seek out the other children their father had sired in the coming year—together.

The door suddenly opened. Had he knocked? He didn't think he had.

"Gauge! I thought that was you." Nina threw her arms around him, crowding him close. She felt good. But not in the way she might have a couple weeks ago. Now she was as dear to him as a sister. Or the best friend she'd once been. And was again.

"Merry Christmas," he said quietly.

She looked happy. "Kevin said he'd heard someone on the porch. I couldn't believe my eyes when I looked out the peephole." She took his hand and led him inside. "Just having you here makes it a merry Christmas, indeed." She closed the door against the cold. "Babe? Guess what the storm blew in?"

Gauge braced himself. He and Kevin hadn't exactly parted on good terms. In fact, his friend would probably not be happy to see him again, turning up like a bad penny on this, his first holiday with his wife.

But Gauge had come to understand that his friend's final words rang with truth: If he wanted something good in his life, then he had to work at it. And he was now ready to put in that work. So whatever the other man hit him with, he was determined to weather his way through it. Because this time, he wasn't going anywhere.

Kevin rounded the corner from the living room and stopped before entering the hall, a box of matches in his hands.

Gauge tried to read his expression. He didn't see anger. Surprise, yes. Exasperation? No.

"Hey," he said awkwardly.

"Hey, yourself." He allowed Nina to help him shrug out of his jacket, taking the bag of gifts he'd brought along. Just a couple of items he'd picked up during his trip that he thought they might like. Things for the house.

Gauge stepped closer to Kevin, overriding his awkwardness, and hugged his friend. "Merry Christmas."

Kevin stood rigidly. But Gauge couldn't judge him on that. Kevin had always been ill at ease with displays of affection.

Gauge merely held fast.

Finally, Kevin put his arms around him, too, and they hugged. Really hugged, for the first time in a very long time.

Kevin chuckled and pulled back. "I didn't think I'd ever say this, but it's damn good to see you, Gauge."

"Same here," he said. "Same here."

GAUGE WASN'T SURE what he'd expected, but it certainly wasn't what transpired. He hadn't even dared hope the evening would go as well as it had.

Was it possible that once you committed to a plan, things only got easier?

Or was it the holiday that cast a sentimental glow on the threesome as the evening progressed?

After a casual dinner, they sat in the living room, Nina and Kevin on the couch, Kevin with his arm around his wife, Nina's hand resting on his knee. Gauge sat in front of the fireplace on an ottoman, the three of them talking like the past ten months had never transpired.

"Oh, this has been so nice," Nina said, as if reading his thoughts, smiling first at Kevin and then Gauge. "Just what I needed to shore me up for tomorrow's visit to my parents'." She patted Kevin's leg. "Thank God I no longer have to go to these things alone."

Gauge poked at the fire. "I thought your grandmother made the gatherings livelier."

Nina grimaced. "She's the reason things are going to be especially tense. She's bringing her 'boy toy,' as she insists on calling her movie-usher paramour."

Gauge laughed. "Paramour. Now there's a word you don't hear enough in songs."

Kevin rubbed his wife's back. "Or in general. I vote that we make a conscious effort to bring it back."

Nina smiled. "I think it's best if we just leave it where it lies."

The three laughed, enjoying the moment.

"Speaking of paramours…" Nina said, leaning forward and pouring more wine into their glasses on the coffee table. She handed Gauge's to him. "Anything to report on the romance front, Gauge?"

He turned back to the fire and took a sip of his wine, pretending to ignore her question. He caught their shared glance out of the corner of his eye.

"On that note," he said, getting up from the ottoman, "I think it's time we called it a night."

They protested, but didn't put much heart into it. It was obvious the couple wanted to be alone.

Besides, there was someone else he wanted to see so much he ached with the need of it.

Nina got up first, coming to hug him.

God, she felt good. Like a fresh spring shower.

"I'm so glad you're back home, Gauge."

"Me, too."

She kissed him on the lips. A brief, friendly peck.

"Hey!" Kevin said.

Gauge released her and they both saw that he was

smiling. If there was any wariness lurking in Kevin's eyes, Gauge couldn't spot it.

And for the first time in a long time, he relaxed completely.

"I'm just going to clean up and leave you two to say goodbye." She kissed Gauge again and gave him a quick hug. "Merry Christmas, big guy."

She collected the plate of cheese and crackers they'd all but demolished and disappeared into the kitchen.

Gauge led the way to the foyer, Kevin clapping him on the shoulder.

"It was good to see you, buddy," Gauge said. "Felt like old times, didn't it?"

"Yeah. Yeah, that it did." Kevin reached to take something out of his back pocket. "Here. Nina and I wanted to return this to you."

Gauge recognized the return address of the law office he'd had draw up the ownership transfer papers. He opened the flap and saw the contract torn into small pieces.

"Don't say anything," Kevin said. "You're our partner and best friend. We'd like you to stay that way as we rebuild."

Gauge shook his head and then gave him a man hug. "I love you, man. And I love that wife of yours, too."

Kevin chuckled. "Yeah, well, just so you remember that she is my wife, then we're all good."

Gauge grinned as he shrugged into his coat and opened the door.

"Hey?"

He looked back at Kevin.

"You got somewhere to go?"

Gauge braced himself against the cold night air. "Yeah. Yeah, I think I do...."

21

LIZZIE RETURNED home late from her parents' house, having taken in far more holiday cheer than she could possibly handle in one night.

Not that her family was to blame. They'd all been one-hundred percent their dear, unique selves—divorce papers, teething babies and god-awful Christmas gifts aside—as they honored the longstanding Gilbred traditions of trimming the family tree, singing dirty Christmas carols, and enjoying a late meal that served as a prelude to the one that would come the following day.

All in all, everything had been much more enjoyable than Lizzie would have thought. So much so that a couple of times she nearly forgot about the gift waiting for her at home.

Nearly.

Truth was, her mind repeatedly returned to the box throughout the evening, wondering what it meant. Why would Gauge send her his guitar?

Slipping her boots off just inside the door, she put on her slippers, grabbed a glass of club soda from the refrigerator to settle her stomach, then went into the family room and started a fire.

Long minutes later, Ella's voice flowing over her, she sat down on the sofa and pulled the guitar into her lap.

As her sister, Annie, had taken joy in pointing out, she'd never been musically inclined. Growing up, she'd rather have a book in her hands than a musical instrument. But merely holding the guitar made her feel as if she were somehow closer to Gauge. Connected.

She pressed her fingers against the neck and strummed her thumbnail over the strings. She made a face and tried again.

Hands appeared from behind her. She stilled, the scent of fresh winter air filling her senses. Her breath exited in a soft rush as Gauge slid his fingers down her arms and then over her hands, placing his face next to hers.

Lizzie felt so overwhelmed with emotion that it took every ounce of restraint she had not to let go of the guitar and turn and pull him over the back of the couch on top of her, making up for the time lost.

Instead, she allowed him to play it out his way. She closed her eyes, rubbing her cheek against his, feeling whole for the first time since he'd left Fantasy. Left her.

"Your back door's unlocked," he said quietly.

She licked her dry lips. "I know."

He positioned her fingers on the neck, pressing them down with his, then guided her other hand farther down the strings. The chord they struck sent tremors of need quaking through her.

"I missed you," she whispered.

She thought he might not respond. Then he said, "Funny. I felt you with me the entire time I was gone."

Warmth spread across her chest like an ink stain, just as pervasive, just as permanent.

Gauge slowly lifted the guitar and placed it on the floor next to the couch and then drew her up to face him, her kneeling on the cushions, him still standing. She stared into his eyes as his gaze raked her face and neck and breasts.

"God, you're so beautiful," he murmured, cupping her face in his hands and rubbing his thumbs over her cheeks, his focus moving from her eyes to her mouth and then back again as if he couldn't look his fill. "There wasn't a moment that went by that I didn't ache for you, Lizzie. Ache for this."

He kissed her softly, lingeringly.

"And this."

He kissed her again.

Lizzie's eyes fluttered closed as she curled her fingers around his wrists, where he gently held her head still.

He rested his forehead against hers. "I've thought about this moment. What I might say. What apologies I should make—"

She pulled back and pressed her finger against his lips. "Shh. There are no apologies. Not anymore."

He stared deep into her eyes. "Yes. Yes, there are. I don't ever want to hurt you like that again."

The image of them on the hall floor, Lizzie fighting him, Gauge holding her still...the two of them having desperate sex, emerged in her mind.

She looked down at his T-shirt, leaning her forehead against his chin. "It took you hurting me to understand how very much I've come to care about you."

He tipped her head back with a finger under her chin and kissed her. And kissed her again. Languidly, thoroughly, sensuously.

"I think I'm falling in love with you, Lizzie."

The back of her eyelids burned and he became a handsome blur.

He smiled slightly. "Those aren't words I'm used to saying. But I promise that it won't take what we went through for me to say them again."

Lizzie did what she'd been longing to do and pulled him over the side of the couch until he lay on top of her, pressing her into the cushions with his welcome weight.

She swallowed thickly, surprised by the rush of emotion that had nothing to do with the holiday and everything to do with the man she cradled between her legs. "It seems crazy, doesn't it? I mean, I don't think either one of us was looking for love, but…" She trailed off. "We've found it, haven't we? You and me? When we weren't looking, it crept up on us and grabbed us—"

"By the balls?"

She smiled, thrusting her hands under the back of his T-shirt, reveling in the hot, silken feel of him against her palms even as she pressed her sensitive breasts against the hard wall of his chest, wanting, needing to be closer still. "I was going to say unawares, but, hey, balls works."

He smiled and framed her face with his hands again,

as if he couldn't believe he was there, that they were there, looking at each other.

"I don't know what tomorrow will bring, Lizzie." The dark shadow she'd grown used to seeing eclipsed his eyes and she knew a moment of fear. "I can't make promises I don't know I can keep." He kissed her, pulling her bottom lip into his mouth, the shadow moving on, affection taking its place. "I'm going through a lot of changes. Changes I think your loving me has set off…"

Lizzie took in his every word, desperately wanting to believe him, wanting to give herself over to him fully, completely. Not just with her body, but with her mind and soul.

"And I probably have no right to ask you this, but…"

She suddenly found it impossible to breathe, her heart pounding against her rib cage.

"Will you consider being my woman?"

She searched his face and then his eyes. His tortured, dark, fathomless eyes. Exploring the planes of his face with her fingertips. "On one condition."

He waited.

"That you promise to be my man."

Epilogue

June, six months later...

IF ASKED A YEAR AGO where he would be now, Gauge
never would have said in the backyard of Lizzie's
parents' house with her siblings, their significant others
and children, celebrating the official signing of her
parents' divorce papers with a blowout family barbeque.
Lizzie tried explaining the situation to him since Bonnie
and Clyde Gilbred appeared to be a couple in every way,
and apparently had no plans to part ways except on
paper, but he didn't get it. More importantly, he felt no
need to get it. So long as they and their family were
okay with the situation...well, he was coming to accept
that was all that mattered.

With the officially unofficial toasts out of the way,
everyone had drifted to different areas of the yard.
Gauge sat holding his guitar on a stretch of thick grass
under an old maple tree complete with requisite tire
swing. Lizzie's niece, Jasmine, lay on her belly in front
of him, her arms propped under her chin, her eyes huge
and adoring. Her younger brother Mason tried out his

new walking legs, his understanding of sibling rivalry growing as he untied Jaz's shoes and generally poked at her for reaction's sake only. Their three-month-old brother snoozed in his stroller nearby, quiet for the first time since the festivities had begun a couple of hours earlier. Lizzie's brother, Jesse, and his new wife, Mona, were sitting on a bench nearby. Lizzie's parents and her sister, Annie, and her husband, Roger, were still gathered around the table on the deck where they'd all eaten.

Lizzie's family made him think of his own expanding role in the Gauge family. His nephew, Thomas, had received a little sister in March, and Lizzie had driven down to Arizona with him to help welcome the chubby bundle of joy into the world. Gorge had been genuinely happy to see him, and Gauge intended to make sure that no Gauge born in his lifetime went without love and the solid foundation that could only be built by family.

Lizzie turned her head where it rested against his thigh, reminding him of the biggest change in his life.

Funny, but he had the feeling that if he'd taken a logical approach to their relationship from the beginning, he probably never would have moved into her mammoth house, would have believed the contrasts between their lives too great. Insurmountable. Instead, he'd followed his heart. And found himself watching her blossom from an uptight trial attorney who favored designer-label black turtlenecks and slacks to a more relaxed woman whose clothing choices ran more to colorful sundresses and all things soft and sexy. They were still designer labels, but the fact she was lying in the grass without concern for stains was proof she was willing not only to meet him in the middle but also enjoy the journey every step of the way.

Or should he say every orgasm?

He grew hard just thinking of their hot sex life. He'd never wanted a woman so much. And with each passing day, it seemed incredible to him that he should want her more, not less. And knowing she returned the sentiment blew his mind.

Then there was Nina and Kevin. He'd felt like a man on death row being given a reprieve when they'd allowed him back into their lives. That alone was enough to be thankful for. But to have Lizzie bond with them, as well…it was more than he could have dared hope for. They met up with the other couple at least once a week, enjoying good food, good conversation and, more importantly, one another.

With the help of insurance monies and the close-knit Fantasy community, BMC had celebrated its grand reopening last month, bigger and better than ever. Although, at Gauge's insistence, the music store was now on the other side of the bookstore, putting Kevin between him and Nina's café…just in case.

Human nature was a funny thing. He understood now that it wasn't enough to resist temptation, but it was necessary to ensure that temptation, period, was made less available. Which meant going home directly after sitting in for a night with local bands. Passing on accepting pretty, flirty music students. And allowing the part-timers at the store to attend to customers who might have at one time turned his head.

It was bad enough that once or twice he'd entertained the possibility of him and Lizzie sharing more than friendship with Nina and Kevin….

He caught the dangerous thought and forced it out.

He didn't deserve what he had. He knew that. But he intended to make sure that at some point he would be worthy of what fate had brought to him.

He finished playing "Puff the Magic Dragon" with a flourish, eliciting wild applause from Jaz and even her brother, who appeared not to know why he was clapping but happy to do it just the same.

Lizzie shifted her head to look up at Gauge. He reached down to cup her beautiful face, grazing the pad of his thumb against her plump bottom lip. Instantly her pupils dilated and her breath exited in a soft sigh.

Damn, but he didn't deserve her. He tangled his fingers in her hair. But so long as he had her, he was going to take complete advantage.

"More, Gauge, more!" Jaz cried.

He didn't take his gaze from Lizzie's sexy face. Mmm. Yes. More, indeed….

* * * * *

Silhouette Desire kicks off 2009 with
MAN OF THE MONTH, *a yearlong program*
featuring incredible heroes by stellar authors.

When navy SEAL Hunter Cabot returns home for
some much-needed R & R, he discovers he's a
married man. There's just one problem: he's never
met his "bride."

Enjoy this sneak peek at Maureen Child's
AN OFFICER AND A MILLIONAIRE.
Available January 2009 from Silhouette Desire.

One

Hunter Cabot, Navy SEAL, had a healing bullet wound in his side, thirty days' leave and, apparently, a wife he'd never met.

On the drive into his hometown of Springville, California, he stopped for gas at Charlie Evans's service station. That's where the trouble started.

"Hunter! Man, it's good to see you! Margie didn't tell us you were coming home."

"Margie?" Hunter leaned back against the front fender of his black pickup truck and winced as his side gave a small twinge of pain. Silently then, he watched as the man he'd known since high school filled his tank.

Charlie grinned, shook his head and pumped gas. "Guess your wife was lookin' for a little 'alone' time with you, huh?"

"My—" Hunter couldn't even say the word. *Wife?* He didn't have a wife. "Look, Charlie…"

"Don't blame her, of course," his friend said with a wink as he finished up and put the gas cap back on. "You being gone all the time with the SEALs must be hard on the ol' love life."

He'd never had any complaints, Hunter thought, frowning at the man still talking a mile a minute. "What're you—"

"Bet Margie's anxious to see you. She told us all about that R & R trip you two took to Bali." Charlie's dark brown eyebrows lifted and wiggled.

"Charlie…"

"Hey, it's okay, you don't have to say a thing, man."

What the hell could he say? Hunter shook his head, paid for his gas and as he left, told himself Charlie was just losing it. Maybe the guy had been smelling gas fumes too long.

But as it turned out, it wasn't just Charlie. Stopped at a red light on Main Street, Hunter glanced out his window to smile at Mrs. Harker, his second-grade teacher who was now at least a hundred years old. In the middle of the crosswalk, the old lady stopped and shouted, "Hunter Cabot, you've got yourself a wonderful wife. I hope you appreciate her."

Scowling now, he only nodded at the old woman—the only teacher who'd ever scared the crap out of him. What the hell was going on here? Was everyone but him nuts?

His temper beginning to boil, he put up with a few more comments about his "wife" on the drive through town before finally pulling into the wide, circular drive leading to the Cabot mansion. Hunter didn't have a clue what was going on, but he planned to get to the bottom of it. Fast.

He grabbed his duffel bag, stalked into the house and paid no attention to the housekeeper, who ran at him, fluttering both hands. "Mr. Hunter!"

"Sorry, Sophie," he called out over his shoulder as he took the stairs two at a time. "Need a shower, then we'll talk."

He marched down the long, carpeted hallway to the rooms that were always kept ready for him. In his suite, Hunter tossed the duffel down and stopped dead. The shower in his bathroom was running. His *wife?*

Anger and curiosity boiled in his gut, creating a churning mass that had him moving forward without even thinking about it. He opened the bathroom door to a wall of steam and the sound of a woman singing— off-key. Margie, no doubt.

Well, if she was his wife… Hunter walked across the room, yanked the shower door open and stared in at a curvy, naked, temptingly wet woman.

She whirled to face him, slapping her arms across her naked body while she gave a short, terrified scream.

Hunter smiled. "Hi, honey. I'm home."

* * * * *

Be sure to look for
AN OFFICER AND A MILLIONAIRE
by USA TODAY *bestselling author Maureen Child.*
Available January 2009 from Silhouette Desire.